AF237555

Noah Fakier, Dr. Lutz Knoche

Driven by the deep need

Danger:
The advisory function in this book relates exclusively to the evaluation and evaluation of bisexuality. About unpublished case studies by Dr. Lutz Knoche, Noah Fakier wrote erotic stories that he put into writing with a lot of imagination. We assume no responsibility for the sexual practices described in this book, for any damage that occurs during the reenactment. Everyone is responsible for themselves. In particular, the use of condoms in the erotic scenes was not explicitly mentioned for dramatic reasons. In many cases, however, they must be used.
If you are unsure, get advice.

Manufacture and publishing
BoD Books on Demand, Norderstedt
ISBN 978-3-7534-6224-0

To the authors

The author Noah Fakier from Berlin writes homoerotic and bisexual love stories. His message is: With the eyes of love, all people are beautiful and unique. No matter where they come from, what gender or age they are. It is universal bliss and therefore a driving force in our life. In his stories, eroticism, and passion play just as natural a role as feelings, longing, adventure, and humor. His drawings on these topics, which he shows in many stories or published as calendars and drawing portfolios, are now enjoying increasing popularity internationally. His books "The Secret Tales from 1001 Nights" and "Lust and Emotions" will also be published in English in 2021 and the folder "Men I" became a bestseller in his publishing house. For the book at hand, he has brought out the drawing portfolio "Der Liebesreigen". https://www.noahfakier.eu

The author Dr. Lutz Knoche In his book "Human Traumata Part I, Global Coming Out", Lutz Knoche from Berlin takes the view that people have neither been exclusively monogamous nor heterosexual since their development. The book is currently published in German, English, and Italian. All human beings have evolutionary dispositions, both physically and emotionally, that are designed for sexual, diverse life. Monogamy and the predominant heterosexual way of life are for Dr. Knoche a temporary abnormal development. https://www.lutzknoche.com

Just because most people are heterosexual and monogamous today doesn't mean it's in their nature. Rather, these behaviors and thought structures are trained. It is just not the case that every person can freely decide which path to take in fulfilling their sexual desires and in love. Rather, his decisions are shaped by false established norms and beliefs that are thousands of years old. Since his birth, he has been exposed to these influences through family, society, religion, laws, and culture. The true nature of the diversity of human sexuality is therefore not related to itself by most, for fear of exclusion, and is often suppressed.

Bisexual experiences are often dismissed as slip-ups. This is particularly dramatic as many reports confirm that bisexuality has been the dominant form of sexuality in the animal kingdom from the very beginning. This is also the case with human development. Your today's desires, fantasies, and urges are a product of evolution. Quite natural and therefore beneficial for human development. Evolution itself is always directed towards development. Only humans are the only living beings that can consciously oppose evolution. In doing so, he often disrupts his development opportunities. This has happened massively through the sexual teachings of the religions. For hundreds of thousands of years, people lived their sexuality freely and openly. We weren't monogamous or straight. Religion then puts us in a sexual straitjacket. That was unnatural and led us to a collective trauma to this day. Even today it still shapes our beliefs and prejudices. Even if most of them are no longer religious at all. But the false teachings about sexuality that were spread back then are often still present, often without our being aware of where it came from. This has many negative effects on our quality of life and development. I write about this in detail in my book Human Traumata Part I Global Coming out.

Everyone should freely determine their path and be recognized in society on an equal footing. And certainly not because of his upbringing and social influences he should doubt himself. To date, only a monogamous marriage is promoted, which has been shown to make many people unhappy in the long run. There are many other ways of love and social coexistence. But in education, culture, and the media, for the most part, the old, false norms and prejudices still prevail. Our ideas and thoughts are shaped by them. Even if they are wrong, many people are still firmly, sometimes even fanatically, convinced of their correctness. I felt this when my book Human Trauma Part I was attacked. But more and more people are questioning these norms.

Sexual upbringing will change, culture will keep opening up and old prejudices will be broken down. This is the natural (divine) evolutionary development of sexual diversity. That cannot be stopped in the long run. I am convinced of that.

Noah Fakier, therefore, breaks out of the currently prevailing false moral concept of our society in his stories. It shows how exciting and wonderful love can be in all its diversity. I know his magical forbidden stories from 1001 nights and I am very happy that he has also prepared my bisexual stories in this book as an author. I would look at more such books, films, plays and lots of other things. To wish.

Dr. Lutz Knoche

Table of Contents

Drawing portfolio "Der Liebesreigen"
- Miniatur excerpt 1-

1. The love dance

"Good morning Leo," I heard half asleep as someone spoke to me in a soft voice. I was lying in bed. The tiredness still kept my spirit trapped in the arms of Morpheus. So I just blinked a little. I saw a young man sitting next to me on the bed. He was naked. When he got out of bed, a small bum beamed at me with half-open buttocks. But only as long as it was directly in line with my field of vision. I saw delicate downy hairs in its furrow. With an irresistible urge, I felt the desire to run my fingers through his furrow. But since he was moving away from me, I could not reach him. So I looked after him curiously. I only saw him from behind. He had black hair, a broad shoulder that rose like a V to a narrow waist. Then followed a small firm bottom, under which two muscular thighs were to be seen. He had a youthful and slim male figure. In addition, a very smooth, delicate light brown skin. As he walked across the room, the muscles of his buttocks tightened. That looked very provocative. I blinked after him until he disappeared behind a door. I got a little sad when he was gone. But then I heard the sound of a shower. Aha, he was in the bathroom, I thought. The monotonous sound of the water and the reassuring knowledge that he hadn't gone made me sleepy again. My eyelids closed as I grunted softly with satisfaction. In a half-dream, I saw this beautiful naked man. That excited me. My member slowly rose to full size and finally stood stiff on my stomach. I enjoyed this rising excitement in this wonderful dream.

Suddenly I opened my eyes wide because I realized: This is not a dream! Where was I? Who is the young man who got out of bed naked? And why was I happy about it? I woke up suddenly and looked around the room. I was in a hotel room. I got up quickly, ran to the window, and looked out into the street. I was familiar with this place. I was in the castle hotel. But how did I get here, and in such a situation? Panic spread inside me. That was new to me and at first, I didn't know what to do about it. I felt more helpless than ever in my life. My memory had gaps and I tried to reconstruct yesterday's day bit by bit. At first, my thoughts somersaulted and I didn't know what had happened. But then I pulled myself together. I tried to calm down by breathing evenly. That helped me. Over time, I calmed down. My thoughts sorted themselves out and soon I could remember yesterday.

Yesterday was Saturday and I said goodbye to my wife and two children in the morning. As planned, they drove to my parent's country house over the weekend. We all wanted to ride together. But the day before, an important client came to see me at the architects' office that I opened three years ago. He handed me a pile of papers. "I want to buy this property. Since there are still more interested parties, I urgently need an opinion from you by Monday. "He explained to me. It was an important customer. In this situation I couldn't say no. That's, why I wanted to prepare the required report over the weekend. As a result, the plan to go to my parents' house with the family came to nothing. But we didn't want to postpone the planned visit.

The parents had prepared for our visit and were looking forward to being able to be with their grandchildren again for two days. And the children were already very excited and talked about it all week. The parents had a house by the forest, a large garden, chickens, rabbits, a cat, and a dog. It was a little paradise for both of us. So this time my wife Sophie drove with the children without me, to the parents in the country.

When I said goodbye to them on Saturday morning, my heart felt a little heavy. I hadn't seen my mother and father in a long time either. I grew up safe and happy with them.

For me, they were the best parents in the world. I was grateful to them for that. I still enjoy being with them today. I was also looking forward to seeing my old school friend Kai again. We were best friends back then. After finishing school, we parted ways. Still, we stayed in touch. Every time we saw each other it was like we'd only seen each other yesterday. I called him:

"Kai, hello, unfortunately, I can't come to my parents today. That means we cannot meet. I'm very sorry, but I got an important job. I have to work on the weekend. " What a shame, I was looking forward to it. If it doesn't work, then next time. But don't let me wait that long for you again this time. "He replied. "Yes, we'll see you soon. I promise you. Next time I'll bring more time with me. "I added. Then we said goodbye.

I would have loved to go with you today. So I looked wistfully after my family as they slowly moved away from me the car they were sitting in until it disappeared from my field of vision. Then I ran straight into the house. I took the customer's documents home with me so as not to lose any time. So the pile of papers lay on my desk in the study. I looked through them and rated them. In the end, I had done the work faster than I thought. I finished it in the afternoon. My wife had already called me and confirmed the arrival of my parents.

When I was standing in the living room afterward, I asked myself: When was the last time I was home alone? I didn't remember anymore. Most of the time, when I got home from work, the whole family was already there. The thought of going after them briefly flared up in me. I would be there in the late evening. I loved my family, but at that moment I was ultimately happy to be alone for a while. Especially since I couldn't meet my friend Kai either. He had invited me to his home that afternoon because he was going on a journey afterward. So I gave up the idea of going after them. Instead, I opened a bottle of red wine and poured myself a glass. First I raised the glass and looked at the ruby red color of the wine in the light. Then I smelled it with relish. It smelled fruity and a little sweet. I liked that because I loved sweet wine. Then I sat down in my comfortable armchair and listened to the silence. Then I raised the glass again and said, "For good." Even if I was alone, I wanted to at least toast with my family and my friend in my mind. Then I read the book "Human Traumata Part Global Coming Out." It was a compelling book and so I kept pulling it out to read a few sections. It was an adult education book. But I would also give it to my son and daughter to read by the age of 13 or 14 at the latest. As I read it today, I thought of my friend Kai.

We were thirteen years old when we played together in the hay barn. Suddenly I saw that Kai had built a tent in his pants. "What about you?" I asked, looking down at this unmistakable bump between his legs. I think I've become a man. I woke up last night. My penis was stiff and my pants were all wet. " Show me what does it look like when it's stiff? "I asked. Kai carefully pulled down his pants. Suddenly a hard club jumped out. At first, I was frightened, but then I became curious. "What is that? That looks exciting. "I said and then I reached for it. Immediately the limb in my hand twitched. And Kai groaned. That made me unsure and I gave up on it again. But Kai said: "Touch him again. That was very nice. "So I did it. Now I was no longer frightened. On the contrary, I let it twitch vigorously in my hand and marveled at the enormous power this thing had with it. I also saw in Kai's face how he made an exciting grimace and moaned in the process. "Oh yes that's nice. Go up and down a little more with your h, and. "He asked me. I had never seen him like this before. So I did him a favor. His excitement didn't leave me indifferent and I felt very weird. Finally, his hard member twitched strongly again. He groaned loudly and then the semen came squirting out of him. That was the most exciting thing I had ever experienced. "That was madness." I exclaimed happily. "You can say that." Kai answered a little exhausted. I never thought that there could be anything more exciting that day. But I was wrong about that. After a short while, Kai looked at me in astonishment. "You also have a tent in your pants!" He exclaimed in amazement. "Yeah, I got so weird when I saw you aroused. I think I have a stiff penis now too. Do you think I'll be a man now too? "I asked him. "Come on, pull your pants down. Maybe you can still experience this feeling of madness today. That would be super cool if we both became men on the same day. "Kai replied excitedly. So I pulled my pants down too. Immediately he grabbed my aroused member. He took it firmly in his hand and kept going up and down with it. I thought I was going out of my mind. What was that? That was incredible. I groaned with excitement. And could hardly stand it. I now moved my hard club in his hand by sliding my pelvis back and forth. So that my member moved even more strongly in his hand. Faster, faster, I shouted excitedly. "And shifted wildly to and fro. But it soon came over me. The semen slowly pushed up my penis. For a moment I thought to lose my senses. But at the last moment I caught myself again and squirted out my first love, juice tremendously. This is how I experienced my first overwhelming climax. My whole body twitched. Then I collapsed, exhausted, and lay in the hay, all four people stretched out from me. "Oh man, that's awesome. Do you mean that it is always like this? Kai exclaimed enthusiastically, but also a little insecure. "I guess so. Why shouldn't it be like that in the future? "I answered.

That day was so exciting and beautiful. So were the following years. We were crazy about it and never missed an opportunity to enjoy ourselves this way. As blood brothers, we swore never to part. But sometimes things turn out differently than you imagine at this age. When we finished school I went out to study. Then I moved to Berlin and Kai stayed in my hometown.

As I read the book, I thought about him and the hay barn. Gradually the excitement rose in me. My penis started pumping and got bigger and bigger. With every twitching movement, a strong shiver of happiness shot through my body. I loved this period when my penis slowly inflated to full size. That gave me wonderful long-term enjoyment. My body was already wrapped in this blissful veil without a will, so I lay back with relish, spread my legs, and just let it happen. Today I was undisturbed again and had a lot of time to savor these hot feelings. So I floated on a lustful cloud of bliss. I had put a hand in the crotch and gently caressed my ever-growing bump. After the entire space in the tight pants was filled, my wand began to twitch vigorously. It hadn't reached full size yet and wanted to create more space. I endured this dramatic, exciting fight in my pants for a while. After a while, however, I couldn't take it any longer and wanted to free him from his confinement. My mighty member should stand majestically up on me. Only he and my hand should be the center of my life for a while. Oh, I will catapult myself slowly and with relish into bliss until after a long time it comes over me tremendously, close to me. Sophie had been busy preparing for the trip for the past two days and was tired that evening. So a lot of semen had built up in me. Today I wanted to let it squirt out of me wastefully and incessantly. I wanted to squirm my body voluptuously and moan loudly. Nobody heard it today. This idea is slowly driving me crazy. Every cell in my body was jumping around in circles with relish and getting faster and faster. Orgasmic anticipation had completely taken over me. I couldn't take it any longer and grabbed my pants to open them.

I was just thinking, today I will once again make ample use of Sophie's dildo for myself. I have twice the pleasure and can satisfy my lust for as long as I want. Hopefully, she didn't take him to my parents' house. Suddenly my stomach started to growl. It didn't stop. It got louder and louder and the wonderful feeling of excitement grew weaker and weaker. Does it have to be right now, I thought angrily? Then it occurred to me that, apart from breakfast with my wife and children, I hadn't eaten anything that day. So the wine worked quickly and I was tipsy. It is high time to finally eat solid food because with a growling stomach I won't be able to enjoy my hot feelings either, I thought. So I put it off until later.

Since it became too quiet in the house over time, I decided to go into town to have something to eat. I felt a joyful expectation at the thought of finally eating a kebab again. Sophie didn't eat anything like that. It was the best opportunity to do something I felt like doing without my having to worry about anyone. I felt comfortable with this thought and decided to enjoy my little freedom. After the wine, which I had drunk copiously, I left the car. Since it was getting late, I took the subway and drove to my favorite kebab stand. The train was the shortest way to get there, but once again the route was closed and I was forced to change trains twice to get to my destination. Therefore I was late.

When I finally got there, someone started closing the shops just then. As I got closer, I recognized him. It was the young man who always greeted me in a, particularly friendly manner whenever I was at the kebab stand. Although he looked young, he was the boss here. We have often exchanged a few words when I was with him. I noticed that he always prepared an extra-large portion for me: "Here's your special doner kebab." He would say every time and smile at me. Perhaps it was his friendliness that kept me coming back to this booth. Because of that, I sensed a chance to get my kebab from him tonight. Now he noticed me. He saw how I ran to him in a hurry and waved to him from afar. So he waited until I was with him. "Would you like anything else?" He asked smiling when I stood in front of him. As friendly as he looked at me, I suspected that he recognized me, even though

I hadn't been there for a long time. "Yes, I'm hungry and today I wanted to have a kebab again. The subway was down, that's why I'm late. Please don't let me down now. I was looking forward to your special kebab. "I answered, still a little out of breath.

The young man, who, although a bit dark-skinned, was certainly of Turkish descent, like most of the people who run a kebab shop, beamed at me with his dark brown eyes and said friendly: "Well, I won't let you starve to death. We men have to stick together. "With this answer, I immediately felt connected to him, because we were two men. "But come back, because I'm going to close the kiosk now. You get your special doner kebab. "He said and laughed.

I was happy and quickly ran behind the kiosk. He opened the door for me. I entered. "My name is Omar." He said hello. "And I am Leo," I answered. After we introduced ourselves, he immediately started preparing the meal. "I've already prepared something because I haven't eaten anything either. It's nice when I don't have to do this alone.

Let's have a cozy meal together. Sit down already. The food is coming soon. "He said and set the table for us. He quickly set a small table with meat, salads and snacks, cutlery, napkins, and candles. It looked inviting and I was touched by the way he tried to conjure up what was almost a romantic atmosphere for us. During dinner, he talked without a break and asked me a lot of questions. I found his curiosity and the way he beamed at me and gazed benevolently a little unusual but also flattering. "Do you have a girlfriend?" He asked and I replied "Yes, I have a wife and two children. But they went to my parents' house for the weekend. " Oh, you look so young and you already have two children?" He asked, astonished. "I'm still young too." I flirted with him a bit. "Yes, you are and very pretty." "But so are you." I returned the compliment and didn't even know why I had said that in the first place. But this young man had such a natural way of handling compliments that I found nothing in giving him one back as well. Especially since he looked very pretty. After we had eaten, he got up from the table. As he stood so directly in front of me while I was sitting, I noticed that he had a rather large bulge in his pants, which was inevitably visible to me in my field of vision. He wore tight jeans in which the large bump was particularly evident. At that age, you are full of energy and have problems. Especially when you've just eaten well and are feeling good all around, I thought. "Is there anything else I can do for you?" He asked with a smile. I replied, "Thank you, I am completely satisfied. I liked it very much. " Well then I'll clear the table."He said. I felt like there was a slight disappointment in his voice. Did I say something wrong? Was he trying to imply with this question that he wanted to be with me a little longer? And I idiot rebuffed him unintentionally, I thought. I got up quickly and helped him clear the table. When we finished, I felt sad. I found it difficult to part with him.

He was very friendly and personable and I felt comfortable with him. So I suggested to him: "You gave me such a warm welcome. I would like to invite you for a drink when you have the time. " Thanks, I have time for you,"he replied happily. He quickly locked the kiosk and we strolled towards the main street. On the way there, I said to him: "I thought you had an appointment with a friend today, because of the huge bulge you had in your pants after dinner." He smiled and replied: "You need to think about that don't break. That's when I'm feeling really good. Doesn't that happen to you sometimes too? " Yes, it does."I answered a little thoughtfully. After we had had a meaningful conversation about our best pieces, everything was clear between us. Funny, I thought. I've never spoken about it to a man I only met two hours ago.

After a few minutes, we were on the main street. It was now half an hour to midnight. On this warm evening, the street was full of people. All the seats in front of the restaurants were occupied. There was a lively and exuberant atmosphere. "Many are enjoying this wonderful summer night today, and it didn't seem like any of them would be getting up anytime soon to offer us their seats," said Omar. "Yes, then we'll have to walk a little longer. But after the plentiful meal, that's fine for me. "I replied. So we strolled further down the main street. A little later we came to a bar that looked very inviting from the outside.

Omar said, "Come on, let's go in here. There are also a lot of gays in here, but the bar is cozy. Or do you have something against homosexuals? " I don't."I answered him coolly and was a bit curious. I had never thought of going to a gay bar before. Now that we were standing in front of it, I felt a little queasy in my stomach, but I didn't let it show. Omer looked at me a bit uncertainly as if he didn't want to believe that I don't mind going to a gay bar. "Come on, let's finally go in," I said and opened the door for him. As soon as we entered the bar, several men greeted Omar with a hug, and since he had introduced me as a friend, they greeted me warmly as well. My slight discomfort was quickly gone after this open and friendly welcome. Immediately afterward I was given a drink by one of the group. Only after the second whiskey did I realize that I had invited Omar. So I quickly ordered the next round for him and his friends before someone else beat me up again. That was the start of binge drinking because everyone in our group felt compelled to give a new round.

I saw men kiss in public at the bar, but nobody minded. Over time, I found that quite normal. I looked around the bar and it occurred to me that there were men from all over the world here. There were Europeans, Africans, Arabs, Turks, and Asians and everyone got on well. It was the colorful picture that I loved so much in this city. And here everyone was united in friendship and warmth.

For a moment it flashed through my head that if the gays, no matter what skin color, get along so well, then it is better if everyone was like that, at least bisexual. I was shocked to realize that I had spoken this thought out loud. The group I was standing with immediately got on. One said euphorically and already quite drunk: "You are right. There would be only one flag in the world. The rainbow flag. "One of our group of Arabs pointed out: "But that might not be ideal either. The women become unhappy and there would be hardly any children. "To which Omar replied:" Who says that only men can be gay? And besides, most of them would be bisexual anyway and will continue to be with women and have children. "One African added:"

Perhaps there would then be many extended families of several men and women, where each one exchanges his feelings with the other as he likes can. "One asked:" But what if a man doesn't care about other men? "Well, something like that already exists today in all parliamentary groups. They are tolerated, as they are now. "Answered the next. Then a lively discussion developed that I had unintentionally started. I was a little happy that my opinion had such weight in our group. That made me feel very close to them.

Omar was always by my side. When he noticed that I was already very drunk and that an African from a distance was constantly smiling at me with his dark brown skin and beautiful white teeth, he took my hand and led me to a cozy place at the bar. It was only dimly lit and we felt undisturbed. I was happy to finally be alone with him. Suddenly he kissed me with the tongue. For a moment I was shocked, but then I quickly found pleasure in it. Men kiss well, I thought. Omar kissed passionately and tenderly at the same time. When he realized I liked it, he pushed his body against mine and I felt our crotch warmer. The throbbing in his pants kept getting stronger as he pressed closer and closer to me as he kissed. Such a passionate hug from a man was new to me. It was different than back then with Kai. It aroused me. I lost my last inhibitions and let my lust run free. When he felt this, he groaned softly. I automatically slid my hand over his back and landed on this tight bottom, which I had already checked out in the kiosk when he was preparing the meal. What a hot cracking ass he had, I thought, as I kept running my hand between his buttocks and gently pinching it. He whimpered softly and slid his tongue down my neck, which increased the excitement in me. "Come on, let's go," he whispered.

He came very close to my face. I felt Omar's lips and tongue against my ear. A shiver ran down my spine. "Yes." I breathed excitedly and also as if casually, touched his adorable little ear with my lips. Briefly, he pressed his body closer to me and I felt the warmth in his crotch. Then he pulled away from me and took my hand to lead me out of the bar. But I didn't want to part with him. So I pulled him back to me and kissed him. He groaned softly and said desperately, "Come on, let's go somewhere else. Where we are undisturbed. "I felt a slight, fearful tingling sensation. As a precaution, I quickly bought a bottle of whiskey at the bar, which we took away. I intended to use it to drown my last fears. The exciting games at the bar and the cuddly devotion of this beautiful young man had overwhelmed me so much that I didn't want to stop now.

Outside the bar, he kissed me again, in the middle of the street. But at that moment I didn't lose any thoughts about it. "Where do you live?" He asked. I thought: It was getting late and the subway had stopped running until the next morning. Only the night bus was still running. It would be over an hour before we were with me. Omar had excited me so much that I could hardly stand it anymore. I couldn't and didn't want to wait any longer. I looked at him and saw from the look on his face that he was just as impatient.

I was already so horny for him that I would have gone anywhere with him. So I looked around desperately looking for help. There was no park nearby. I saw a hotel across the street. "Let's go in there," I said and he agreed. In the room, we then continued to drink whiskey, and what happened afterward? I can only remember it in fragments. I only know that he suddenly stood naked in front of me, undressed me and we went to bed. The lying position finally clouded my brain. After that, the images from my memories were just blurry.

As I was reviewing the last day and trying desperately to remember more details, Omar came out of the bathroom freshly showered. I was still standing naked by the window with my back to him. I stopped as if petrified. And didn't turn around. He came to me. Got behind me and pressed his body to my back. Then he threw his arms around my stomach from behind and clung tighter. We were both naked and so his member was now between my buttocks and began to get bigger. "It was nice with you tonight," he whispered in my ear. He came very close with his mouth again, so that his lips tickled my earlobes again. Then it struck me like lightning. Suddenly I remembered how he had penetrated me during the night, with his limb already stiff again. Even if it was a bit strange at the beginning, I was soon overwhelmed by an unexpected lust.

I also remembered shouting, "Don't stop! Don't stop! "When I stood at the window and felt him, I automatically opened my furrow again and he slowly pushed his member into me again. I groaned with delight. Now it was moving inside me. That was awesome! And I was grateful that I was able to experience it again in full consciousness this morning. What was happening inside of me? Are these feelings overwhelming? With every movement of his hot hard member, he gave me indescribable feelings of happiness, which spread like waves through my whole body and got stronger and stronger. I held on to the window frame, pushing my bum forward so he was able to get deeper into me. I groaned softly and raised my head. It got warmer inside me. Suddenly he stopped moving. I was a little frightened: should it be over by now? But he said, "You go on" I was relieved and happy that there was a sequel after all. Now I was moving my bum back and forth. I was driven harder and harder with ecstatic excitement until his member in me twitched vigorously and he roared. I also groaned because these violent movements in me triggered a wave of lust. What just happened there? That was the most exciting thing I have ever experienced, I thought. But Omar wasn't done with me. He pushed his member out of me, now stood at the window, and bent down too. In doing so he opens his furrow what a sight! This young man has a nice bum, I thought, and my heart pounded with excitement. Then he said: "Now it's your turn. You weren't able to do it last night. Penetrate me and take me. "

When I heard that, I couldn't believe my luck. I quickly stroked the wonderful bottom he willingly held out to me and ran my hand between his firm cheeks. In doing so, they kept opening up. Then I carefully massaged his opening with my middle finger. His whole body started shaking. "You're driving me crazy," he cried. "Come on, put him in, I can't take it anymore." With this request, which he called softly to me in an almost pleading voice, I could no longer hold back and slowly pushed my hard member into him. It was tight, warm, and damp in it. At that moment I couldn't have imagined a more beautiful place. When I was completely in him, Omar lost all inhibitions. He was now vigorously moving his abdomen back and forth, moaning loudly and shouting: "Oh, I love you, go on, harder, deeper!" I held onto his slim hips with my hands, because I was afraid to lose one's balance. He rode so hard on my member. As I was used to, I put my hands to my chest. There I felt two large, hard nipples, which surprised me a little. I didn't know that they can get so big and hard with a man. When I ran my hands over her, he shouted: "Yes, that's awesome!" Since I liked to play with nipples and knew my way around them, I took them between two fingers and rubbed them. That made him wild and he shouted: "Tighter, tighter!" At the same time, it rode excitedly on my member. I pinched his warts tightly as I rolled them back and forth between my fingers. Omar was beside himself and jerked his upper body back and forth as if he was not able to decide in which direction to move it first because of the excitement. But I had his nipples firmly under control so that he could no longer escape me. At the same time his bottom, in which my member was stuck, was jumping back and forth faster and faster. I also fell into breathtaking delight. I have never experienced such a wild ecstasy in another person. It was a firework of the senses. Then a tremendous climax rose in me and I roared. After that, we were both exhausted and lay down on the bed. After a period of exhilarating contentment, I checked my watch. It was already afternoon and my wife and children were home in two hours. I had to leave and part with Omar. I told him that and he asked: "Will we meet again?" "Yes, of course," I answered. He gave me his phone number before we said goodbye.

On the way home, I felt the happiness hormones still dancing through my body that had exploded inside me during my recent meetings with this wild young man. I was happy and had the feeling that the passengers in the subway were looking at me in a particularly friendly manner. As if they were looking at me that I had just had a happy time. But I wasn't embarrassed. On the contrary, I smiled and enjoyed that bliss within me. Now I was looking forward to Sophie and the children. When I reached into my pocket, I felt the slip of paper with Omar's phone number in my hand. I have to get rid of it as soon as possible, I thought. For me, it was a one-time thing and at that moment I didn't think about contacting him again. When I got home, I took a shower straight away to remove the traces of this insanely exciting encounter that weekend. After that, I waited for my family. Meanwhile, I thought again of Omar, whom I had seen today in all his horny beauty. My member twitched happily at the thought. Not now. Wait a minute, I thought. Finally, Sophie and the children came back from the weekend vacation. My six-year-old son and five-year-old daughter were already running to the house. I came towards them and when they saw me they shouted with joy, "Papa, Papa." I crouched down and they fell into my arms. "I am happy that you are with me again. Was it nice with grandma and grandpa? "I asked, hugging them tightly to me. "Yes." They both answered. Then I got up and I greeted my wife, who had been waiting for my children to let go of me. I hugged and kissed her. Maybe a little too passionate here on the street. She looked at me a little puzzled, but her eyes shone. "So, did you have a nice weekend?" I asked her. "Yes, but I missed you," she said. Then we ran into the house and my daughter first told me in detail what she had experienced with grandma and grandpa. Her little snout no longer stood still. Sophie and I smiled at each other. We knew her. Unless she was interrupted in her flow of speech at some point, she would go on talking until she went to bed. That's why Sophie said to her a little later: "Now you've told Papa everything. Come on, help me unpack and get the things into your room. "Since she not only talked a lot but also liked to move, she went straight to work and disappeared into the nursery.

"How was your weekend?" Asked Sophie when we were alone. I said, "You know I had a lot of work. But I went to my kebab stand in the evening. " I thought so, "she said with a smile. I watched her stand by the kitchen cupboard and put away the jam my mother had made herself. Except for her short haircut, which

I found very pretty, Sophie hadn't changed much in the eight years we were together. She was athletic and her small breasts were a perfect match for her slim body. I didn't understand why many men found big breasts so horny. That probably came from the Stone Age, when they meant fertility and enough food for an infant. Sophie looked at me and noticed that my thoughts were elsewhere. "What are you thinking about right now?" She asked me. "Your breasts and how beautiful they are," I answered her. She smiled, "Do you find them that beautiful?" "Oh, yes they are perfect," I replied. "That pleases me. I haven't heard anything like that from you in a long time. " That's why I'm telling you now"and we smiled at each other.

When we had finally put the children to bed in the evening and were alone, I kissed them. "I love you," I said and she returned it with a passionate hug. We undressed and faced each other naked. She walked around me once and looked at me. "You are still a tight young man and you have a firm ass" and pinched my buttocks. I moaned slightly, turned to her, and hugged her tightly. My member got harder and harder and slowly rose pressed against her body. That excited her and we lay down on the sofa. I was lying on top of her and she opened her legs for me. "Wait," I said to her. "I want to spoil you first." Then kissed her breasts and sucked on her nipples. Sophie moaned softly. "Oh, what are you doing with me today? That feels good. "After a while, I pushed my body down. First kissed her stomach and then I put my face between her legs and led my tongue through her vagina. Always deeper and faster. Sophie turned her body back and forth.

"What are you doing?" She asked excitedly again. I do not answer her and I also believed that she did not expect an answer. I just continued to spoil them with this wonderful game. Again and again, I massaged her clitoris vigorously with my tongue. Suddenly she lifted her pelvis and groaned loudly. It got wet between her legs. She had an orgasm and then collapsed satisfied and exhausted. It was a long time since I had brought her to the top of her climax this way. I lay down on her and kissed her face, glowing with satisfaction, tenderly. Her forehead, eyes, nose, and chin.

My member was still hard on her stomach. When she calmed down a bit and noticed my excitement, she said: "Now it's my turn. Lie on your back. "I followed her instructions. Then she kissed my neck, chest, and nipples. "Suck it," I asked her. She did this for the first time. It excites me. I couldn't help thinking of Omar and could understand his excitement. Even if my nipples weren't as big as his, it made me feel very pleasurable too. When Sophie noticed how it turned me on, she sucked harder and I moved my body under her with excitement. Then I indicated with a slight pressure on her shoulders that she should go deeper. Immediately she crawled down with her body on me and got to my member, which was already excited and began to pump. Now she slowly pushed it into her mouth as deeply as she could. According to my feelings, it took a sweet eternity until she had completely absorbed him. She repeated that over and over again. I started to moan and felt like an orgasm was looming in me. Now she pushed it no longer deep inside but licked like mad at my acorns. That finally got me into a frenzy. My body started to shake and I jerked my head to the left and then to the right again. Finally, it came out of me and it didn't want to stop because I felt her tongue licking wildly on my glans while my semen spurted out of me in powerful bursts. That prolonged the orgasm and I had to moan loudly. But unfortunately, that also came to an end at some point. She came upstairs and we kissed tenderly.

"Would you like a glass of wine?" I asked after I had recovered something and she nodded. "Don't get dressed," she said to me. "I want to see you walking around the room naked with your crack ass." I got the wine from the kitchen, ran provocatively through the living room and she whistled softly after me. I stuck my butt forward a little and wiggled it. "Do you like it?" I asked. She laughed. When I came back with two glasses of wine, she was already sitting on the sofa in her negligee. I then put on my boxer shorts as well. Our glasses rang when we toasted and then we drank from this sweet and tasty wine.

We recently started planning our summer vacation with the children. We hadn't yet set an itinerary. So we took the opportunity to rest and talked about it that evening. "Would you like to have a look at some brochures?" Asked Sophie. "Yes, but you will get it now," I said, and she looked at me with a smile. "Of course, my love, I will do everything for you." She got up and ran provocatively through the room while I watched her. Under her see-through negligee was nothing more than bare skin. That got my hormones going again. I ran to her and tenderly bit her neck. I knew it never failed to affect her. She bent down to get the brochures from the cupboard. She stretched her butt out towards me. "Wait stayed like this," I whispered and stroked her bottom. Again I thought of Omer's little crack butt. I reached under her dress and ran my hand between her buttocks through the furrow. She spread her legs. So I could slide through her crotch and tenderly gray her labia from behind. Then I ran my middle finger through her vagina and felt the clitoris, which I then rubbed.

It got wet again in her vagina. My member was now ready to continue making love with her. I slowly inserted it into her vagina from behind. She groaned. When I was completely inside of her, she began to move her abdomen, stronger and faster. I didn't move because I wanted to watch her for a while and enjoy her horniness in peace. But I couldn't stand it for long and then adjusted to her movements. In the middle of the room, I kept sticking my hard member into her like crazy and we were both no longer masters of our senses. I didn't come that quickly while she was overwhelmed by another orgasm. "Come on, kneel on the sofa and put your arms comfortably on the backrest," I said to her. She took this position quickly and I slid my member back into her from behind. But this time between her buttocks. When I moved violently inside her, it aroused her more and more. She pushed her bottom towards me. And shouted: "Yes, yes, go on. That's awesome. "A short time later I lifted her upper body, came forward with my hand, and put it between her legs to get to her clit, while I continued to take her forcefully from behind. When I noticed that an orgasm was looming, I rubbed her hard with excitement and ran my fingers deep into her vagina. I felt her whole body shake and Sophie gasped and whimpered as I moaned. Again she got wet and I came into her at the same time with loud moans.

Now we were completely exhausted. I sat on the sofa and Sophie laid her head on my lap. Suddenly the door opened and our son came in. He stood sleepily in the room and said: "It was so loud. That's when I woke up. "And saw that neither of us was wearing anything. He had often seen us naked in the bathroom or on the beach, but in this situation, here in the living room, it had to be unusual for him. I said: "Sorry Jonas that we woke you up. Papa and Mama loved each other and sometimes such loud noises arise. "I ran to him, picked him up, and carried him back to the nursery. There I put him in bed and he fell asleep again right away. When I got back into the living room, Sophie was standing there smiling at me. "It is now time for us to go to sleep too," she said. She came to her and hugged me. "It was wonderful today. You have changed somehow. But I like that very much, stay that way. "And I immediately thought of the note that Omar had given me with his phone number as a farewell. I tore it up and threw it in the wastebasket in my study.

The next day I took the snippets out and put them together. Then I wrote down his phone number in my notebook. I thought for a moment: what if a park had been nearby that night. We would have moved there for a quick action and then parted ways. Drunk as I was, I would probably hardly remember it and would not have a phone number. And I probably wouldn't have gone to the kebab stand out of shame either. But as it was, I had a wonderful memory and could call Omar at any time. The nonexistent park was our fate. I had to smile at the thought.

Sophie and I continued to have many pleasurable hours in the days that followed. I realized that our love life had become rather monotonous over the years. Now we enjoyed it again imaginatively and more often. We were loving each other like we haven't done for a long time, and not just during sex. I read again in my favorite book "Human Traumata Part I" "and although I had already read it, I felt now, through my own experiences, that what I had experienced with Omar was something completely natural and normal. I remembered the conversation in the bar. There I had accidentally uttered a sudden thought out loud. And I noticed how responsibly and sensitively the men in the group talked about it. In retrospect, I admired her for it.

A few days later I called Omar. "Hello, how are you" "Hello Leo, I'm glad that you are calling. I have often thought of you "Omar recognized my voice immediately and I was happy about it. "How does it look like? Can we meet? "I asked him. "Yes, whenever you want." He replied, "I would like to have a special kebab from you again." But I'm open from 11:00 a.m. to 10:00 p.m. If you come before or after, then we would have more time for each other. " Then I'll be with you tomorrow at 9:00 because I don't want to miss your lookup. „And laughed. "I'm glad, but come on time. I'll prepare everything so that we can eat right away and then have more time for ourselves. "He replied with a laugh. „Maybe there is also a starter to greet you before dinner because I already have a real craving for it?" I asked back. "If you talk like that, you're driving me crazy already. The chocolate bar for the starter is just noticeable and is waiting impatiently to be nibbled. Stop it, otherwise, there will only be a starter and a follow-up and we won't have time for anything else. " No, no in-between we should fortify ourselves with your delicious dishes, the better it tastes afterwards."I afterward all, I'll make sure that everything you want is in abundance." We ended our conversation and I was looking forward to tomorrow morning with him.

One day later I was at the kebab stand at 9:00 a.m. sharp. I ran straight behind and knocked on the door. Omar opened it and beamed at me. "Come in." He said. He took my arm and quickly pulled me into the kiosk, pressed me against the wall and we kissed passionately. We hugged our bodies violently. We quickly undressed and picked up where we left off. I felt our hard limbs pressing against our bellies. This aroused me and I moved my body to rub them together hard. I held Omar tightly around me. "No, no stop, that's too much," he exclaimed excitedly. But I couldn't stop and pulled him closer to me and rubbed myself harder on him. Omar gave in to his fate. "Yes, I love you, that's so nice with you." He said now. A short time later I felt how his member twitched violently and his warm love juice poured between our bellies, while this wonderfully horny young man gasped and moaned incessantly.

It excited me so much that I also felt an orgasm announcing itself in me. When Omar noticed this, he quickly knelt in front of me and took my member in his mouth. "Yes, give me his love juice," he said excitedly. It only took a few seconds and it came to me. I almost lost the ground under my feet in the process. When we had calmed down a bit, I said: "I needed this quick shot. Don't be angry. "I'm not angry. „He replied," It was fantastic. It's just that I've never seen anything like that. "And he kissed me. " But now I'll quickly prepare the food first."

I sat down so that I could keep an eye on him while I was cooking. We stayed naked and I keep starting on his hot ass. Every little movement of these firm buttocks in the narrow kitchen I registered with delight. That was not hidden from him either. He kept looking at me and beaming at me. Each time he said, "I'll be ready in a minute." After ten minutes he came with the meal and set the table. But I stayed seated and didn't help him. I wanted to watch his naked slim body move. And it was a treat to see him lean over the table to place the food on it. I thought he did it for me particularly long and delightfully because he noticed my looks and it aroused him. His member grew larger. "You're driving me crazy again." He said and looked at me lovingly with his radiant dark eyes. "It's not my fault if I like you like that," I replied with a smile and was happy that I was able to arouse him so much with just my looks.

A little wondered and thought. How attractive a man can be? Especially when you have experienced how awesome and lustful it is with him. Unlike with a woman, but no less exciting. Then we ate together what he had prepared. It tasted wonderful and for a short time, I forgot my instinctual desires and lost myself in the physical pleasures. While we were eating, he asked about my wife and children and I asked him what he had been up to in the past few days. Our conversation did not last long. When we had eaten the warm meat, I was already sitting at the table with an erection again. When I realized that it was the same for him, I asked, "What do you think, can we eat the salad later?" Without answering, he quickly came to me, immediately laid me on my back, and kissed me. When he was lying on top of me, he was rubbing his slim, aroused body firmly against mine again. "But now I want to get in your cute bum." I said quickly before we were no longer able to part. "Oh, you can savor this lust whenever you long for it," he said. Sat down on me and slowly pushed my hard member into his already moist, warm, and narrow opening. He immediately fell into ecstasy and rode on me. First I watched him. I saw his magical face beaming with happiness and his slim, muscular body, how he sat on top of me and moved excitedly. But then I was ready to lose my composure myself. I closed and rolled my eyes and started moving my pelvis up, down, and in circles so that he could feel me inside him as much as possible. I felt it getting hotter inside. The second time, as always, I had more stamina. After a while, I asked him to squat like a puppy. He gladly took up this position. He stretched out his hot, now hot and open ass towards me. "Come on quickly. I'm sharp. "He said. But I enjoyed the sight and stroked it. Run your hand through his damp furrow and tickle his hole. "More, more, he exclaimed, very excited. I need this now. You've already made me so wild. "I ran my tongue through his furrow and lingered there by his hole. Immediately he pressed hard these wonderful buttocks, with the wide-open buttocks, into my face and rubbed it. He groaned without a break. I couldn't breathe anymore and with a heavy heart, I had to get out of it. Now I redeemed him and lead my member into him. "Oh, yes, he exclaimed, relieved." And then there was no stopping him. I saw this incredible spectacle. How his horny body writhing and trembling beneath me with excitement rode on my member. For a while, I tried to stop the orgasm that was beginning in me to experience it longer in this indescribable ecstasy, but soon I couldn't. It came over me and another orgasm catapulted me into the highest bliss. Omar looked tired afterward and I thought that I wouldn't feel it inside me today. But it had been so nice with him that I didn't care either. We then ate the salad and drank a glass of wine. But he quickly recovered. "Now you should feel me inside you." He said excitedly. "If you still can." I replied. "And if I can!" He laid me flat on my back again and we kissed. I thought he wanted to get inside me, it ran through my head, and already had the thought to turn around. But then he took my legs and pushed them all the way forward. My butt opened wide and came up. Now he lay down on me again and pushed his member into me. In this position, we could kiss while he was inside me. It's like being with a woman. Only that I am lying down and feel a limb in me, I thought enthusiastically. But I was unable to think further because I passionately lost my composure during this. First I tried to support him with my body movements. But it was difficult in this position. He had to deal with it on his own. Which he did with great zeal. I put my arms back. Then I just let him do it and surrendered to lust in wonderful bliss. After a while, I felt his member twitch violently as it discharged inside me. There was no sound from Omar and he rode on inside me. What was going on? Was I wrong? But suddenly he opened his mouth and from it came a loud deep moan. Then he collapsed on my body. He was trembling all over. I gently stroked his back to calm him down. After two minutes he was breathing more calmly. Then looked at me beaming and grateful and kissed me tenderly.

"Believe me, I've never even come close to experiencing anything like you. I am so happy. "He said to me. I hugged him tightly for a moment. Then we got up and got dressed.

It was getting late now. He had to open his kiosk in half an hour. For this, he still had a lot to prepare. I helped him clear the table and then we said goodbye. "I'll get in touch with you," I said. He nodded and looked at me a little sadly. I understood that. I would have loved to stay too. But I went home again and he didn't know when we would meet again. Of course, he was sad. But then his eyes light up again. He kissed me goodbye and said, "I'll always think of you until the next time." "Me too," I answered. I was completely sweaty after this experience and decided to go home first to take a shower and put on new clothes. My wife and children weren't there at the time. In the shower, I thought of Omar. How should it go on? He had apparently fallen in love with me and I loved him too, but I also loved my wife and children. That was a complicated situation. The first thing I wanted to do with the next meeting with Omar was to talk about how he imagines it. And then we'll see, I thought.

A few days later Sophie told me that she would have to go on a business trip in the next week. "I couldn't refuse that, Leo. It's too important. "She apologized to me. She worked in a publishing house and had to go to the Leipzig Book Fair because a colleague got sick. This trip lasted a week. "But I've already spoken to your parents. You can bring the children to them during this time. " But you could have talked to me beforehand. Maybe I would have liked to take care of her during this time. "I replied. "I said yes, you can take her to your parents, you don't have to." She replied. "Sophie, you know exactly when you have offered them this, then they are excited with joy and the children are looking forward to it too. No, now I'm bringing her to them. "After thinking about how I would spend the week without a family, it occurred to me to take the opportunity to calmly reflect on our future with Omar. So I called him and asked if he would like to take me on vacation for a few days. At first, he didn't say anything. "Hello Omar, are you still there!" I called over the phone. Then I heard him ask in an excited voice, "Is that true? Are you planning to go on vacation with me? " Yes, I told you. „I answered. "Of course I want that, Leo!" He called joyfully and loudly over the phone. I laughed and said, "Not so loud. My eardrum bursts. " But I had to say that out loud so that you could hear it."He replied with a laugh. After we had discussed everything, we prepared for our little vacation trip. It was four days that we could spend together. Omar found a substitute for his kebab stand, which was not a problem among Turks. I have often admired this mutual help and support between them.

I then took the children to my parents. They were really happy that their grandchildren were with them for a whole week, and it was like a vacation for both of them. It's nice to have a family like that, I thought. After saying goodbye to my parents and children, I picked Omar up and we drove to Lake Stechlin. I had rented a bungalow for us there. He stood alone in a large garden that ended directly at the lake. This gave us a small private beach and was undisturbed. We got there in the early afternoon. First, we unloaded the car. It was fully loaded because I had already bought a lot of food and drinks for the next four days. This gave us more time to ourselves and did not have to go shopping all the time. Omar had also packed groceries because he was planning to cook Turkish for us. When I saw that, I said, "Well, you've brought a lot of work with you. I'll think about how I use this time while you're cooking. "Omar laughed and replied:" You don't need to worry about that, I'll find something for you to do. "After we had stowed everything away, we stood in the Bungalow and looked at us. Only now did we realize that we were alone for four days and nights. This created an overwhelming feeling of happiness in us and we fell into each other's arms. After that, we didn't part anymore.

That lasted until the next morning. The breaks in between were short, because not long and one of us started to spoil the other again. We just couldn't leave each other. Even when Omar was cooking the meal that evening, he had to interrupt it. Even during this time, I couldn't leave him. His naked body was a magical attraction for me. So I caressed and kissed his hot bottom so that he lost his composure and opened up. "Was that what you thought of when you said you'd find something for me to do while you cook?" I asked excitedly. "Come on, put it in." He asked me. "But you have to cook the food," I said hypocritically.

"Until you have it in me, there will be no food, you devil. First, you make me hot, and then I should continue to cook. "I laughed and gladly granted his wish. We continued these games until the next day.

In the late morning of the following day, I sat down with him at the lake and asked him. "What do you think, how should we go on?" I fell madly in love with you and I want to be with you every day. "He replied.

I said, "But I have a wife and two children who I also love very much. Do you have a girlfriend? " Yes, I'm engaged. My family arranged the wedding a long time ago. She also lives in Germany and looks very pretty. I don't have much to fear from her, however. She seems to be more interested in women, which I saw in my relationship with her friend. A few weeks ago I happened to see them having fun together. We're getting married, but it looks like I have my peace from her. I just need to give her the freedom she wants. I'll be happy to do that. "He told me. I said, "It's a little different with me. I love my wife and sex with her and I love you ... "I don't mind if you sleep with your wife too, as long as it's not another man, "he interrupted me. "I have to have sex with Adiba now and then. It is compulsory to father at least one child, otherwise, there will be trouble. Maybe we'll find a house and all move in together? Then you can father the child with Adiba, "he said for fun. I laughed: "No, my dear, you perform this act alone if your tradition so wants and you have to stick to it. Besides, they would certainly be very beautiful offspring that you fathered. "Omar smiled. "I can well imagine having children. But with you. "And he laughed. I replied, "That doesn't work, but if there are four of us living together, then we can raise them together. I think it's better for children when they grow up with several adults. "He looked at me with shining eyes and asked, "Do you think we could all live together?" Let's see. „I said a little thought because a plan was already developing in my head. "Oh Leo, that would be great!" Omar exclaimed excitedly and kissed me. "Wait, it's not that far yet. I have to think about how to bring this plan closer to Sophie. And that won't be easy. You and Adiba must get along with her. And I also want to get to know your fiancéeée first. Four people would get their money's worth. " Except for Adiba."Omar said a little thoughtfully. "Oh, I think Sophie will take a liking to her in time. A lot of what I do with her can just as well be done by a woman to bring her fulfillment. "What are you doing with her?" Asked Omar curiously. "I'll tell you later. Now think about what you want to do with me tonight. "Omar laughed:" I don't have to think long. I already have a lot of ideas. But one evening is certainly not enough. A lifetime at the most. " Come on, let's get started quickly. Not that I'll die of old age before I've learned everything you want to do to me. "He got up and took my hand. "Well then let's go into the house. Let's start with this life plan. Everything else will work out. "We quickly ran into the bungalow and didn't get out again until the next afternoon. Despite our frequent passionate gatherings during these hours, we had time to continue making plans for an extended family. Especially since Omer didn't leave me alone with it and started over and over again in between. I explained to him that I have a house and that I am an architect.

This house is large and can easily be converted into a two-family home. That would not be a problem. "A bigger hurdle is to convince Sophie of our ideas about an extended family," I said. "Leo, I would do anything for it if that works!" He shouted fervently.

The four days passed by in a flash. The time together in the bungalow was over and we drove back home. We were a little sad about it. But the plans we had made over the past few days gave us hope for the future. Even if I would miss Omar, I was looking forward to the children and Sophie. The days with Omar had excited me again to the utmost. My body was still set up for pleasurable games. I left the children with my parents for a day longer so that I could spend some alone time with Sophie. When she came back from the business trip, I picked her up at the airport. We beamed and hugged each other tightly.

"I missed you," she said. "I'm also happy that you are back. The children are with my parents one day longer, so we have the evening and the whole night to ourselves. "I whispered in her ear. She smiled: "Then let's go home quickly." When we got to the house, we fell around our necks and kissed. Then we quickly took off each other's clothes. Sophie was overwhelmed by me again and I enjoyed her unrestrained lust. I did a lot of things with her that a woman could have done, and I consciously paid attention to how she got into orgasmic ecstasy. After that, I was sure that she could enjoy sex with a woman. She was a modern young woman and I didn't think she objected in general.

On such lust-filled nights, the heart opens and one often talks about things that require a benevolent ear from the other. So I wondered if I might not speak carefully to Sophie today about the plans I had made with Omar. First, slowly approach it, I thought. But there she came first. "Leo, seriously, what about you? You have changed. For me, very positive, as I said before. But there are reasons for that. You either have a lover or a boyfriend. " How did you come up with a boyfriend?"I asked her in pretend surprise. "Well, you have such a gentle manner, that would somehow suit you. You're not gay, otherwise, we wouldn't have so much fun having sex, but maybe you get something that makes you happy and also revives our sex life. Something I can't give you. "She replied. "What would you prefer then, a lover or a friend?" Think briefly: "I think a bisexual friend. I wouldn't see any direct competition in him. I also believe that you are happy with me and the children. We also give you something that a friend cannot give you. With women it is usually something different, they want the man to themselves at some point. " Well, it's a friend. „I said briefly. Now I had piqued their curiosity. She looked at me in amazement.

"Who is it? Do I know him? How did you meet? Do you love him? " Stop, stop, stop. „I said, not so quickly. It would be best if I tell you everything from the beginning. Then told her the whole story about me and Omar. That doesn't mean exactly everything. I left out the fact that Omar is not into women. But instead, I told him about to his fiancée and that they want to get married soon. She listened understandingly and attentively and then said: "It's nice that we have all become happier."

I had such an instinctive feeling that I had been unconsciously preoccupied for a long time and asked: "You have so much understanding. Do you have any experiences with the same sex? "She replied:" Before, yes. I once had an intimate girlfriend. " And did you like it? „I asked further. "Yes, I liked it, but then I met you and she didn't understand. So for me it was called her or you. I made up my mind for you. " Would you want a girlfriend again if she accepts me?" I don't know. I think the feelings are crucial. "She replied. „You're absolutely right." I took her in my arms, laid her on the bed and we began our next lustful round.

The next day she said to me: "Why don't Omar and his fiancée Adiba over to dinner over the weekend. I would like to get to know them both. "For a moment, I was a little puzzled. It all happened so quickly. Was she really honest with me in her understanding? But I knew her and I knew that she always says what she thinks and wants. So I put my doubts aside and was happy about her openness.

I called Omar the next morning. Because of the unplanned short vacation with him, I had meetings with clients every morning for the following week. That is why we arranged to meet for an hour in a cafe that evening. I wanted to explain to him personally and in detail what had happened. Omar arrived on time and was very excited. "What happened?" He asks, worried. "Did you get in trouble at home?" I smiled and said, "No, on the contrary, my wife is inviting you and Adiba to dinner on Saturday evening. She wants to get to know you. Can you make that possible? " I have to. "He said and asked impressed: "How did you do it?"Now I told him everything and he was also amazed at Sophie's reaction. Yes, he admired her. "Well, I would sleep with her once in a while, if necessary." He said impressed and smiled at me cheekily. "First you see to it that you manage it with your fiancé," I answered and had to laugh. "Don't tell Adiba and my wife about our plan to move in together yet. We have to slowly prepare them for that. "I added."It's clear. But I'm very confident about that. "He replied.

I explained to him: "Today we don't have time for each other, but I have already planned that from now on I will come to you every week on Monday, Wednesday, and Friday in the morning if you want." He replied indignantly: "What does that mean if you want? Why do you say something like that? I'm always really happy when you're there. "We drank our coffee and discussed the weekend meeting. In the end, Omar dragged me to the bathroom, where we were alone, and kissed goodbye. Then I drove back home and waited impatiently for Saturday evening.

It rings at the door. With a little palpitation, I ran to open the door to our guests. Omar and his fiancée Adiba stood in front of me and they both smiled at me. It took my breath away for a moment. Adiba was truly an extraordinary beauty. Now my wife came out of the kitchen and greeted her too. We will accompany you into the living room together. "Please take a seat, I'll be right back."Will you come into the kitchen with me?" Sophie said to me. When we were there, she asked excitedly: "What is that? They are two very pretty people. So with Omar, I can understand you completely. "And she smiled at me. "Okay, but now I have to go back in, we can't leave her alone at the beginning." And I ran back into the living room, where Omar and Adiba were sitting. I was still far too excited to take in Sophie's enthusiasm. "Sorry. My wife needed help in the kitchen. It will be finished soon. "I said. "Where's the kitchen?" Asked Adiba. "Around the corner here." She got up and said, "I'm going to help her." I was about to reply that it wasn't necessary, but Omar took my hand and whispered: "Leave her, it's a tradition with us. A woman is not allowed to sit in the room while another is working in the kitchen. She has to help her. "I looked at him and said: "Nice that you are here."Even if his eyes only flashed briefly, this little moment made my heart beat faster again. A little later the women set the table in the living room. Sophie called the children to dinner. They came running quickly.

They had received instructions from Mama in advance not to be seen until they were called. So they were waiting impatiently in the nursery. Now the time had come and they could finally welcome our visit. First, the big one stormed in. When he saw Adiba, he was nailed to the room with his mouth half-open. She did not have a headscarf on and her long black curly hair fell to her back. She was slim and wore a red tight-fitting dress that came down to her ankles and was embroidered with pearls. She looked like a princess from 1001 nights. When our son still didn't move after

a long minute, Sophie said: "This is Jonas our son."
Adiba looked at him. "But you are a handsome boy.
Hello, I'm Adiba. "And held out my hand to him. He
stepped cautiously to greet her. When he continued to
stare at her and couldn't let go of her hand either, I
said, "Look, there's someone else here. Do you want
to greet him too"and pointed to Omar. Finally, he
came to, ran to Omar, and greeted him too. At that
moment our whirlwind came running into the room.
She was a little late because she wanted to make herself
particularly pretty. So she came running with her
chains around her neck and a small bracelet. She too
saw Adiba first. "Oh, you are beautiful. Are you a real
princess? "She asked. She blushed a bit and replied:
"No, my name is Adiba and who are you?" "I'm
Rosie." She said and held out her hand. Then she saw
Omar: "And who are you?" She asked him curiously
and ran to him. "I am Omar. Sorry if I'm speechless.
But I wasn't expecting a beauty like you here. "Rosie
beamed like a honey cake horse and shook hands with
him.
"So, now that everyone has greeted each other, please
come to the table, the meal is ready," said Sophie. We
all sat down at the set table. While we ate, Rosi kept
looking at Omar and flirting with him, who of course
replied. I knew his look, even if I didn't see his eyes
now, I knew that he had won Rosi's heart with it. Jonas
kept looking at Adiba, who always smiled at him with
her brilliant white teeth and was having a lot of fun.
When we finished eating, Sophie said to the children:
"So now wash your hands, brush your teeth and then

you go back to your room." Rosi protested immediately. "But Mum we have visitors, can't we stay a little longer?" "I wouldn't mind," Omar said to Sophie in a friendly manner. "Well, after 20 minutes, then it's over." We sat down on the sofa and armchairs again. There was no place for the children. Rosi immediately stood next to Omar and began to tell. Omar took it and put it on his lap, which she was visibly proud of. Her little snout held the 20 minutes that she didn't stay still. Omar listened carefully and even asked her additional questions. That means for her that she had a real conversation with him. That was the greatest. Now he had finally won her heart. Our taller sat down on the arm of the armchair on which Mutti was sitting and always looked at Adiba. But just listened to the two women talking and didn't say a word myself. The 20 minutes passed like in a plow. "So now wash yourselves and then off to bed," Sophie said to the children. Suzy looked at Omar and asked: "Will you come and say good night to me?" "Yes, if you wish." He answered. "Well then, see you soon," she called and ran into the nursery. "Shall I say goodnight to you as well," Adiba asked, giving Jonas a friendly look? He blushed and nodded. "Well, see you soon." When he was out of the room, I said to Omar. "The boy is 6 years old. He can't be interested in women yet. "Omar laughed:" How did you get that. Can't you remember your time or were you a late bloomer? " Well,"I said. "It's possible that I was a little late." Sophie looked at me and said, "It doesn't matter.

Everything is right with you, my darling. "At which I and Omar smiled. "So we women go now. We're busy in the kitchen. Should I bring you another beer from the fridge? "Asked Sophie. "Yes, of course." They went off and we got our beer. Then she disappeared again immediately. "Why did they go into the kitchen? Is that something of a tradition with you too? "I asked Omar. "Yes, it is the women's meeting and conference room. All important and unimportant decisions for the family are made there. "Just let them do it. Your wife is very much in order and Adiba noticed that too. They understand each other. "He explained. I said: "And you have already won the hearts of our children too. This is fantastic. You are good with children and you will become a great father. "Omar smiled. "The two of us together will be," he said. "Now that I have met Adiba, is your offer still standing that I can father a child with her?" I asked jokingly. He smiled: "Of course, there is no one more suitable than you. But the way we planned it doesn't matter. "I quickly replied, "No, you have to make it with her. I want to have a child with you. You have already met two fine specimens of me. " That's right, you have two wonderful children and I very much wish that we all get along well, "he said. "The way it started, it can work." I answer,

"Come on, say good night to the children!" We heard Sophie call out. We got up and ran into the nursery. Adiba was already sitting with Jonas and let himself be adored. Rosi sat in the middle of her bed and presented herself in her best nightgown. "Adiba has already said good night to me. I'm waiting for you. "She called when we entered the room. We ran to her and I said: "Now off under the covers." And wanted to put her in bed and cover it. She asked: "Can't Omar do that today?" Then Omar sat down with her, put her on the bed, and covered her. Then he kissed her on the forehead and said, "Good night my princess. Dream beautiful things. "I also kissed her afterward, although I wasn't sure if she had even noticed, because Omar had completely bewitched her. So that she just lay there, smiling dreamily. Then we left the nursery. "I think they'll sleep well today," Sophie whispered to me as we walked out. "Yes, and dream especially well," I replied with a smile.

Then the women disappeared back into the kitchen and we went into the living room. "If I were sure that Sophie and Adiba wouldn't come in for the next lesson, then I would know what to do with you," I whispered in Omar's ear. We hadn't been together all week and in his presence, the wildest fantasies were developing in my head, to which I was helplessly at the mercy. "Stop it, your words are exciting me again," he replied softly. And since I saw that the bump in his pants was getting bigger, I suggested: "Come on, I'll show you the house." And led him out of the room to distract him from his excitement. First I showed him the first floor. The living room, the kitchen, a bathroom, a study, and a guest room were located here. The latter was intended for our parents when they came to visit us. Then we ran into the basement.

I had a craft room there. "Here I mainly make models for my architectural office and nobody bothers me," I said and grinned at him.

Immediately he snapped and kissed me. I pushed him away from me a little. "But we have to be quiet, otherwise you can hear it upstairs," I said in a hushed, excited voice. "Yes, we can do it." He whispered impatiently to me and pulled me tight again. It was in this whisper that we spoke to each other for the first time, which excites us in a very special way. "I'm so horny because we haven't seen each other all week," said Omar. I felt that because his member was already pumping excitedly and always bumped against my stomach. I slid down, undid his pants, and took out this wondrous wand. It was already twitching vigorously in my hand and was about to discharge. Omar didn't move. He had thrown his head up to the nape of the neck and pressed his fist as deeply as he could into his mouth so that no sound came out of him. I quickly took his member in my mouth and slowly pushed it deeper and deeper. Omar was trembling violently and I felt his semen slowly rise. I watched with delight as he shot out of him.

Since he already had his pants down, I said afterward that he should turn around and bend over. "I don't know if I can stay calm about it." He whispered a little fearfully. But then he took off his clothes because he loved being naked and I liked it too. Then he turned his back on me. I kissed his bottom. But today I didn't want him to be too ecstatic with it. He should be able to keep calm. When his rose was wet from my kisses,

I got up and slowly pushed my member into it. "Are you moving now? I standstill. You can better control your arousal and set the rhythm. It'll make it easier for you not to get louder. "I whispered in his ear. He moved slowly and only a little. I looked down at his bottom as he moved back and forth, as if in slow motion. His whole body was tense and trembling all the time. I knew how hard it always aroused him when I was in him. I was therefore aware of how much he had to pull himself together at that moment. That looked so cool and I also used all of my willpower not to move in it. I closed my eyes and just concentrated on the ever-increasing feeling of pleasure that seized me. Omar whimpered to himself and continued to move very little. I thought I was going out of my mind. I was getting more and more aroused in him, but hardly anything happened to ease my and his unbearable tension. I hadn't imagined it to be so carefully and slowly. So I moved a little, but he whimpered a bit louder. So I immediately stopped my activities. Then I continued to watch how he moved his abdomen carefully and heard how he whimpered, pitifully. I no longer knew if it was torture for him or if he liked it. So I asked quietly, "Is it all right?" Oh yes, he replied. "Is that true?" And tried to get confirmation from him again. I wanted to be sure he wasn't saying this just to please me. "Yeah, I wish it would never stop. That's so lovely. To feel you in me. Leave him in me. "He whispered in a broken voice. "Oh, you look so beautiful in your strong excitement. And your heart-rending whimper makes me shiver in joy. "I gave back quietly. This kind of "quiet" union was new to us. Over time, I felt that our two bodies were becoming one. As if we are gradually merging wonderfully.

Granted, it was created out of necessity, but apparently, we had discovered something great. Finally, it came to me and through the continued only slight movements, this orgasm came up in me extremely slowly. That was breathtaking. It then took me a few minutes for my body reflexes to return to normal. Omar was holding me the whole time and caressing me lovingly. "It's all good," he whispered while my body twitched violently at short intervals. I clung to him tightly. He has never been as close to me as he was at this moment. After we had recovered a little, we ran upstairs and sat in the living room.

At 10:00 p.m., the first evening together was unfortunately over. Omar had the job of delivering Adiba back home on time. They weren't married yet, and there were strict rules for a young single girl. So we said goodbye that evening.

After Adiba and Omar left, Sophie and I sat in the living room. We ended this eventful evening with a glass of wine. Sophie was already tipsy. "What were you saying and giggling in the kitchen all the time?" I asked her curiously. "When women talk alone, men shouldn't know all about it." That was the answer I got. "But you left us alone the whole evening." "Leo, don't say now that it bothered you." I had to smile and she saw it. "You see. Adiba and Omar are very personable and beautiful young people. Even though they look so adorable, I didn't notice that they got themselves up for it, like most in the situation. " Well, we're very pretty too, and we don't think anything about it."I said with a smile. "You're right about that." She confidently agreed with me. "I think we are a good match and our children are already excited about them," I said to her. "Yes, that's why I made an appointment to go shopping with Adiba tomorrow in town. So you have to pick up the children from kindergarten. " Oh!"I answered, puzzled. However, she did not provide any further explanations. Which I didn't expect either.

From then on we met regularly in our house and I visited Omar three times a week, as planned. The two women also often met alone in town. Omar told me that Adiba is delighted with Sophie. "I think something is about to happen," he said with a smile. "But Omar our wives are not unfaithful to us," I replied, pretended to be indignant. We looked at each other mischievously and laughed. When they were back with us one evening and we happened to overhear Sophie and Adiba kissing in the kitchen, we ran back into the living room unnoticed. Omar looked at me with a beaming smile and was thrilled: "Leo, I think our plan will work." To which I grinned and replied: "As I know Sophie, it will soon no longer be our plan. She'll take it out of our hands. "We then kissed passionately. Since there were again violent movements in our pants and we moaned softly, we quickly went down the cellar. We had started a handicraft project together as an alibi for our frequent stay there. On the stairs down, Omar didn't let his hand off my bum anymore and stroked it lovingly. I knew what to expect today and was looking forward to it. I took his hand and said, "Come on quickly, let's go down."

When I was in bed with Sophie in the late evening and she had snuggled up to me, I asked her: "So how are you and Adiba going?" "Good, she is very nice." I got the answer. But since she didn't say anything else, I spoke to her. "Sophie, we never wanted to keep secrets from each other. That's why I told you about myself and Omar ..." Yes, but only when I asked you about it. "She interrupted me. "Okay, I'll ask you now. How do you feel about Adiba? " I like her very much and we have an intimate relationship with each other." And, are you happy? " Oh, yes. „She answered. "Do you want to leave me now?" I asked. She looked at me startled: "No! What makes you think that? Do you want to leave me? "I laughed: "Of course not. I love you and I want to spend my life with you. " Me too. „She confirmed and snuggled close to me. "But what do you think if we expand the house and create a second apartment for the two of them. They are getting married soon and need a home of their own. Then we could live together? " The idea sounds tempting. But give me a little time. "And a short time later she asked: "Do you mean that Omar will accept that with me and Adiba? He comes from a different culture, so you might think differently about it. " I think he will accept it. And had to suppress a smile, because I found it amusing to put her under suspicion.

"I'll talk to him." "Good, do that then. But be careful. I don't want this to destroy our friendship. If he and Adiba move in here under these circumstances, then I wouldn't mind. "Sophie said. "Yes, I'll talk to him about it in peace. But I think he will understand. "

I spoke to Omar the next morning and he now wanted to speak to Adiba as well. He made up his mind to tell her all about the situation between him and me, and she asked if she was okay with it. Also about the prospect that they could both get an apartment in our house. After two days, when I was with him again, he burst as soon as I walked in: "I talked to Adiba for a long time. She likes Sophie very much. You too, of course. And she is also enthusiastic about the children. It would be nice for you if we could live together. "He beamed at me full of joy:" Leo, we made it. I love you. "His feelings overwhelmed him and he couldn't move. Only a few tears of joy rolled down his cheeks. So he stood very stiffly in front of me. I took him in my arms and my heartbeat wildly with happiness. Can it be that easy to become happy, I thought.

Omar and Adiba married in the spring of the following year and then moved into the new apartment, which I had built according to their wishes. Our children were completely over the moon and were very happy. Although we had two apartments, we mostly lived together in the kitchen and living room. Sometimes four or three of us shared the bedroom when one of us was not there. As a precaution, I had built a particularly large bedroom with an adjoining whirlpool in the new apartment. Omar was fascinated by Adiba's enchanting charisma when she was with Sophie lustfully. And Adiba curiously watched his overwhelming ecstasy when he lost himself with me. This also brought them closer emotionally and physically. Although his wife stuck to Sophie more and he stuck to me. The way we loved it.

But the two of us continued to have our freedom, which we gladly and imaginatively used. When I was alone in bed with Sophie that evening, she crawled up to me and caressed my bum. Then she said: "Omar also has a hot bottom." "I have already noticed how you like it when you stroke it with your glorified historical expression," I answered and smiled. "Yes, sometimes I wish to be a man then, to take full possession of him, as you do with him." "Yes, my darling, only I can do that," I said proudly and laughed. "So in the next life I want to be a man," she decided. "But maybe then Omar will be a woman." I pointed out. "If he's as horny as he is now, I wouldn't mind that either." She replied and laughed too. "How do you like my bum? Is he that much worse than Omar's? "I asked her. I lay down on my stomach and lifted him. "No, definitely not. You know that I think he's super horny too. "And she caressed him again lovingly."Well then don't force yourself and take it." Because her caresses between my furrow aroused me slowly. Now Sophie became more passionate too and put a finger inside me. I groaned and said, "One is not enough. Take more. "And then we tried out what was possible and it got us both very excited. A little later I sat down on all fours on the bed and shouted: "Yes, that's great.

Now take me. "Before Sophie shouted: " But I can't do that. "I turned my head to her and saw her face looking at me desperately. I suddenly had to laugh and so did she. Our excitement evaporated. We hugged, just kept laughing, and couldn't stop that quickly.

Adiba soon became pregnant and we were all looking forward to the child. It was definitely from Omar. I never went that far with her because I wanted a child from him. At the family celebration on the occasion of my father's 60th birthday, everyone suddenly came and congratulated us. But we didn't know why and were surprised about it. It finally cleared up. Our whirlwind, Susi, had happily told everyone that she would soon have a little brother or sister. We quickly set the facts right in our relatives. And explained that they were our friends.

Later, when we were alone at the party, Sophie said to me: "Basically, she's right that we're having a child. At least that's how I feel. "And I replied: " Of course she is right, but do you want to explain it to our relatives? "She laughed and replied, " Oh, my God, that would be a scandal for her. "And thoughtfully she added: "It's a pity." I took her in my arms and kissed her: "It's not important whether you know it or not. The main thing is that we are happy. There will be a time when everyone can live as they want in public and nobody is bothered by it. Maybe we'll still see it. I think that then many people will live like us and maybe this will lead to completely different forms of coexistence. "Sophie looked at me mockingly and said: " I just hope that you don't come up with other ideas. "I laughed and replied: "No, I don't think so, I'm still too firmly anchored in the old, but wrong, norms about love for that. And the way it is with us, I like it. "

Twice a year, Omar and I, as well as Sophie and Adiba, went on short breaks for a week. We used the time to enjoy our togetherness undisturbed. During this time, the other two took care of the children and of course also had time to themselves in the evening. When Omar and I were on vacation, we sometimes spent hours at the lake or sailed on a boat and enjoyed our togetherness. It was a tradition that we both always went to the Stechliner See. We then experienced the big vacation together with the children. Everyone was looking forward to it. Omar was in love with the children and they used every opportunity to do something with him.

We also got on well with our neighbors. I noticed that his son kept crouching with Omar when we were all together. He looked very handsome and was 19 years old. One day, when we were having a barbecue with our neighbor again and they were crouching together all evening, I felt compelled to remind Omar of what he had said to me at Lake Stechlin. Namely that he doesn't mind if I sleep with my wife, the main thing is not with another man. "Why are you telling me that?" He asked in astonishment. "Well, when I see you and Philipp together like that sometimes, I notice how he adores you. I also notice that you like it. "I replied.

"Oh Leo, you don't have to worry about that. I love you and it will always be like that. "Then he looked at me affectionately with shining eyes and said amusingly:" And if a handsome man is interested in it, then only with you. "Stop it! "I cried and wondered me about the fact that this thought didn't seem completely absurd to me after all.

I later told Sophie about the conversation when she told me she was unsure whether Omar would accept this about her and Adiba. "We saw you guys kissing in the kitchen before. Omar was ecstatic with happiness. So I didn't need to carefully teach him that you guys got so close. " You're mean! To let me wriggle like that,"she exclaimed, pounding me with her little fists. I laughed and held her arms tight. Then I kissed her and we sank into bed. I took it passionately. When we settled down, I snuggled up against her and said, "I love you." "And what about Omar?" She asked. "I love you both with all my heart," I replied. "Me too" I heard Sophie say.

***

Drawing folder "Der Liebesreigen"
- Miniature excerpt 2-

2. On the hill of lust

"Have you been waiting a long time, Max?" Eva called to me from afar. "Yes, a full ten months," I replied jokingly. Eva's grandparents lived here in the village and she has visited them every year on summer holidays since she was a child. Today she had just arrived again and had arranged to meet me at our old meeting point. We played together as children. At first, it was sandpit games, later it was doctor games, in which we carefully explored our physical differences. It was an exciting time as we spent our childhood together every summer. But it got really serious when we were 13 years old. When Eva, as "Frau Doctor", once again carried out detailed examinations on me, I suddenly got strange and shouted: "Stop it" But it was already too late. I got my first orgasm. We didn't know what had happened. I did not have an erection and there was no semen. And I only found out later that it was an orgasm that had thrown me off track. Startled, we immediately stopped the examinations. "Then what is the matter with you?" Asked Eva, puzzled. "I don't know either, but suddenly I got weird," I replied. Two days later I had my second orgasm while I was sleeping and my boxer shorts, in which I was sleeping, got wet. After that, it was clear to me that I had become sexually mature. I told Eva. Since she was the "woman" in my life who had caused the first orgasm in me, we kissed each other on the mouth and decided to become a couple. However, we are no longer continuing the doctor games.

We kissed and caressed. But only up to the waistline. Sometimes we would show each other the genitals because we were curious to see how they would develop year after year. Eva was particularly impressed when she saw my stiff penis. When we were together and she noticed the ever-increasing bump in my pants, she usually asked me to take him out so that she could stare at him in amazement. Once I picked up my member. Then I always drove along and showed her how the semen spurts out of me at the end. Since I groaned when it came to me, she became curious: "How do you feel about it when that comes out of you? She wanted to know. But I couldn't describe it to her so that she could understand it. "You touch yourself down there." That's why I asked her. She did that and stroked her labia. "And do you like it?" I asked. "Yes," she replied but stopped immediately afterward. It must have been a little creepy to her. "Caress yourself a little longer. Maybe you can then feel for yourself what a feeling that is. "I said to her. "I'll try that later," she replied. I thought that was stupid. But since she excluded me from it, I no longer let her participate in my orgasm. We also no longer showed our genitals and I was no longer allowed to stroke her small breasts, which were just developing. So far we had told and shown each other everything, but that has now changed. Nevertheless, we continued to get along very well and were happy when we could be together.

It all started three years ago. We've been a couple on summer vacation ever since. We looked forward to it all year round. Eva lived in Munich. She had invited me to her house several times, but I didn't feel like going to the big city. I felt good in my village and the mountains. Big cities were a horror to me. Even as a child I worked on my parents' farm and at some point I would take it over. My path was mapped out and I felt safe and secure. I couldn't imagine a better life. Despite my 16 years of age, the hard work on the farm made me quite strong, and therefore my figure was masculine. Today Eva had returned to her grandparents' home over the summer vacation. As was our tradition, we met at 3:00 p.m. on the day of her arrival at our old spot on the hill. As always, I had made up my mind to spend a lot of time with her this summer. When she was there on vacation, I had fewer tasks on the farm because my parents knew about our friendship. I got more free time so that I could do something with Eva more often.

As we greeted, we hugged and kissed. "I've missed you so much," she said, and her eyes lit up at me. "I missed you too. I am glad that you are here again now"I confirmed to her. Since we were together, we have met almost every day on this little wooded hill above the village. From there we could see the whole place, the mountains, and the forests. The hill could be seen from the village, but the people there ignored it. For one thing, there was no way to get there. On the other hand, there were just too many more attractive places nearby to hang out. Fortunately for us, because we were there undisturbed. After we sat down on the grass, we looked for a while at this wonderful panorama that was offered to us from up here. Eva and I were here again for the first time this year. So after a long time, we enjoyed the wonderful impressions that nature gave us here in the middle of the mountains. Then Eva told me about Munich. She was very talented and played the violin. So she applied to a music high school and gave me a detailed description of how she had prepared for the audition and how excited she was when she then had to audition. She was then accepted into the grammar school and will attend school there after the holidays. In addition to her normal school schedule, she had 3 hours of music lessons every day after that. But that didn't bother her. On the contrary, she was delighted with it. Her mouth didn't standstill. She kept talking about Munich and grammar school. While she continued to speak, I took the opportunity to take a long look at her. I found that she had changed since we last met a year ago. She wore a brightly colored summer dress and was even prettier. Suddenly she became quiet and said: "You don't say anything." I had to laugh: "If you keep talking all the time, how can I say something?" "Sorry, but you know me." She replied quickly.

Oh yes, I knew her. I had also noticed that the greeting kiss this year was exceptionally passionate. She had her body pressed tightly against mine and that excites me. I've never been kissed by her like this. I thought she learned something new in Munich. But that didn't bother me. It was enough for me when we were together on vacation. She would never move to my village anyway and I wouldn't move to Munich that was clear. So we enjoyed the holiday season together every year. And at that time there was only us. She looked at me and eyed me: "You have grown up." She said. "What do you mean?" I asked. "Well, you already look like a real man. You have got a broad chest, stronger arms, a firm buttock, and a small beard that is already growing. I think your penis must have gotten bigger too. "She spoke about the latter for the first time in 3 years. Now I examined her more closely and noticed that she also looked more mature. "But you've changed too. Your breasts have grown. " Mostly you? „She asked back coquettishly. "Oh yes, you have beautiful breasts. I would like to pick it up again. "Stop it." She said and laughed a little embarrassed. As we kissed, I carefully put my hand on her knee. When I slid my hand a little lower down her thigh and wanted to test, like last year, how far she read it, she opened her legs slightly. This was new to me and I became curious about how far I could go. Carefully and a little uncertainly, I ran my hand up the inside of her thigh and she let it.

I felt like I was in a dream. With every inch that my hand went higher, my heart beat faster. After a short time, I was between her crotch and tenderly caressing her labia through her panties. I couldn't believe it yet that she let me up so far and I was a little dizzy with excitement. She was only wearing thin panties and I noticed that they were getting wet. She had closed her eyes and was moaning softly. When she then spread her legs further, I put my hand into her panties. She had shown me her pussy several times before, but I was never allowed to touch her before. Today was the day. And I didn't even have to seduce her into it, she showed me clearly that she was ready for it herself. That made me feel unimagined because it made me hope that more can happen today. Her pussy was soft and it felt good. I ran my middle finger carefully between her wet labia. She moaned softly. So I kept doing it. Over time, I noticed a little hardening and played on it with my finger. As I knew from books, that was certainly her clit. She whispered excitedly: "Yes, that's wonderful, continue to stroke me there." And took off her panties. Then I lost my last insecurity. We lay down on the grass and I purposefully brought her into ecstasy with ever-faster movements on her clit. Her increasing excitement and her voluptuous moaning excited me now too. There was movement between my steps. My member was pumping excitedly, getting bigger and bigger until it was hard. Inexorably, it bumped into my tight pants with rhythmic movements. Because of this constant friction that it was exposed to, it aroused me more and more and I feared that it would soon come to me and a full load of my semen poured into her. Soon I couldn't take it any longer and released it from its distress. Eva didn't notice anything, the faster I played on her clitoris with my finger, the more aroused she became. She had closed her eyes, writhing her whole body back and forth with excitement and whimpering loudly. At the same time, I now started to walk along with my stiff member with the other hand, because I was increasingly excited by her frenzy. Suddenly there was silence and she was trembling all over. Since I didn't know what was wrong with her, I stopped playing with her and myself and looked a little startled at her.

Afterward, Eva lay on the grass with her eyes closed and a satisfied expression on her face. Everything was in order. She had experienced her first real orgasm and was overwhelmed. When she opened her eyes a short time later, she looked at me beaming and shouted: "That was amazing. I didn't think it could be so beautiful. I saved it for you because I was also the first in your life. "I gave her a long kiss. Then she looked down at me and saw my member, which was still stiff. I wanted to finish it now and continued, as usual, sliding my hand up and down on him. "Stop it, Max, I want to do that today." She said and immediately afterward went to work. My member twitched powerfully, which she liked. Each twitch created a wave of happiness in me that shot through my body. It was much stronger and nicer when she did it and I didn't have to lend a hand myself. But it got better. "Take off your pants and lie on your back." She asked me. I wasn't told twice. So I lay in the grass and enjoyed her caresses on my hard member. First, she did it with her hand, but then she put it in her mouth and pushed it up and down in it. I freaked out. I already had oral fantasies, but I hadn't yet imagined that it would be so hot. Slowly I felt an orgasm building up in me and I could hardly stand it. "Faster, faster," I called. When I did it myself, I got faster and faster. But you don't. So this time it slowly came up in me. My orgasmic ecstasy grew stronger and stronger. I turned my body in aroused tension and roared. I finally reached the top of this incredible climax. When everything was out of me, I lay down on my stomach, completely exhausted. "We have to do that more often from now on," I said enthusiastically. "Yes, if you want." I got the answer. The idea of experiencing something like this with Eva every day made me feel very happy.

Then we lay next to each other on the grass for a while, happy and content. We didn't talk but enjoyed the deep, relaxed satisfaction that was now spreading within us. It felt good to have Eva by my side. After a while she sat cross-legged on my left side, facing me. I was still on top of the book. I hadn't put on the pants.

"I'm so excited about what I've just experienced with you and I can't find peace. Let me stroke you a little. Just lie there and enjoy it. "She said. Eva began to run her hand over my bottom. "You have a very nice butt. I have often imagined what it would be like to stroke and explore it everywhere. And this year it has become even more attractive. "She said." You have a nice bottom too," I replied. "You haven't looked at it yet." "I'll investigate that later," I replied. But now I wanted to enjoy her caresses first.

My best friend Paul always told me that I had a great butt. Whenever we were alone, he stroked it and kneaded it tenderly. In the beginning, I protested against it. Since my protests went unheard, I gave up at some point and left him to Paul for his pats. After a while, I liked it too. Everyone thinks my bum is awesome, I thought proudly and smiled. When I was thinking like that, I didn't notice that I had automatically spread my legs a bit and lifted my buttocks while Eva caressed me. That way she could run her fingers deeper through my furrow. That was so awesome! When she got to the sack through her spread legs and scratched it, everything was too late. I got an erection again but didn't feel like turning around, because then the caresses would stop back there. But that was so nice and I didn't want to do without it now. So I bent my hard member backward between my legs. Eva immediately included it in her caresses. While she stroked one hand up and down my penis with her fingers and now lingered on my bum with the other and tickled my hole incessantly, I moaned louder. I was paralyzed and agitated at the same time. My whole body was trembling with excitement.

"Oh, you're driving me crazy with it. Keep it up. This is amazing. "I exclaimed. Eva lost her last inhibitions and got out of hand herself. She took my member firmly in her hand and drove it violently up and down. In addition, she tickled my hole with her middle finger, always sliding something into it. Involuntarily, I lifted my buttocks even higher, causing her finger to slide deeper into me. Then she always pushed it a little way out and back in again. I gasped and groaned. I could not form words, my mind was no longer able to do so. What was she doing now! She also took her index finger and stuck them both in me and wiggled them in me. I gasped violently. I slid my hand excitedly between her legs. By sitting cross-legged, her labia were wide open. She hadn't put on her panties yet and I immediately began to look for the clitoris in her vagina and then rub it wildly against it. She began to moan and her seated body swayed. Now she was going crazy. Violently she took my member and even faster she ran her two fingers in and out of me. And I supported her with the up and down movements of my buttocks. Now I stuck my finger deep in her hole and wiggled it too, then took the second one. Eva was moaning incessantly now, just like me. Since I only had an orgasm shortly before, I was able to experience this insanely horny feeling for a long time without it coming to me immediately. Eva was wet again in the crotch. She had her second orgasm during this long and wild action.

But I wasn't ready and very excited. So I didn't stop running my fingers into her hole over and over again. She didn't say anything, just kept moaning. But soon I felt a new climax rise in me too. Somehow I had to endure this increasing excitement. Therefore my fingers rotated faster and faster in Eva. My butt jumped up and down like a rubber ball and Eva drove relentlessly in and out of me, while she clasped my already violently twitching member tightly in my hand and ran along with it forcefully. Then it came to me. With a deep dull moan, I discharged myself. And it didn't stop that quickly. Again and again, I felt orgasm-like thrusts that shot through my whole body and made it shake. After a while, I found my peace.

Eva was still moaning and whimpering. I kept my fingers in her and kept moving them around. "Yes, that's so nice!" She exclaimed. Without getting out of her, I put her on her back again. "Today you should also feel this wonderful pleasure that you can bring about with your mouth," I explained to her. I quickly put my face between her legs. Then I slid my tongue through her crevice. When I felt her clitoris, I massaged it vigorously as fast as I could. Eva pushed her pelvis up. In doing so, it opened further. She was beside herself and whimpered. With my tongue, I came deep into her now. After a while, it got wet again and she experienced her third orgasm that day. Then we lay next to each other, totally exhausted. We both looked very happy and loved it. At the end of the day, we decided that we wanted to repeat that as often as possible during this vacation.

We said goodbye for today. On the way home I was still thinking about what wonderful things we had experienced there. If I tell Paul what Eva has done to my buttocks and how incredibly awesome that was, he will not rest until I do the same with him. Although we are the same age and he is taller than me, he still has a boyish figure, but his small buttocks look great and are firm. So I made up my mind to stroke him with my hand now, just as he has been doing me for years. I wanted to give him a taste for it. Because I had my ideas. Maybe there are more options among guys than just going in with your fingers. Well, as long as we don't have any decent girls in the village, we could at least have fun together when Eva is gone, I thought. Smiling and with wild fantasies in my head, I ran home. I noticed that my crotch was twitching again. Well, that could be something, I thought with a smile.

And it was. I had the most exciting vacation with Eva that we had ever spent together.

I gave Paul a taste for it after Eva left. At every opportunity, I put my hand on his bum and patted him. Since it aroused him very much and his limb was getting stiff, I soon told him about my fantasies: "What do you think of it if we press our limbs in the back of the other. I think that would be great. " I've already thought of something like that. We should give it a try. "Paul replied. I had just put my hand on his tight little bottom and always slid along in the middle of his furrow. Now Paul reached back between my legs with his left hand. He pressed hard on my bump. I groaned loudly. "Come on, pull your pants down and bend over. We'll do it now. "I said excitedly. He quickly pulled his pants down and bent down. He held on to a beam. When I saw his bare bum with the furrow open in front of me, I also pulled my pants down quickly. A hard club jumped out. I quickly looked for his hole and pressed my penis on it. When I pressed harder to get in, Paul called, "Hold on, wait. That hurts. You have to moisten your glans first and massage your hole a bit beforehand so that it becomes soft. "I took some spit on my index and middle finger and rubbed it into its opening. "Yes, that feels good. Go on. "Paul whispered excitedly. I felt his rosette soften. "Should I try again?" I asked him. "Yes, but carefully." He replied. Now I spat in my hand and rubbed my glans neatly. Then I start for the second time. I put my hard member on his soft hole. "You push it in so I don't hurt you." I said. He did that now and pushed his bottom forward. I watched as my injection of pleasure slowly disappeared in him. That was so awesome. When I was completely in him, I asked him, "How are you feeling?" "I don't know. It's a bit strange. "He replied." Shall I move?" I asked him. "Yes, do it. Slowly back and forth. "He said. Now I always pushed my member in and out of him a little bit. Its hole was tight and the friction in it excites me a lot. Now Paul began to moan too. "Oh, that is getting more beautiful. Yes, carry on as you like. "He exclaimed excitedly. When I continued, there wasn't much going on for me. I was soon ready and it occurred to me. I injected my semen into it for the first time. I groaned loudly. Paul noticed it and also groaned excitedly. Then my pleasure injection was soft again and slipped out of his hole. "A shame, just where it was cool, it stops again." He said a little disappointed. "You do not have to be sad. We'll do that a lot from now on. "I replied." Yes, but today I'll show you how nice it is when I'm in you too," he said. "Definitely. Immediately if you can. " And whether I can. Just bend over, you should feel me inside you in a moment. Yes, wonderful. Wait, I'll take my pants off completely, so I can widen my legs and open up more to you. "Stop talking like that, or it'll come to me before I'm inside you." Paul cried. After taking off my pants, I bent down and held onto the beam as well. Paul caresses my bottom tenderly and said enthusiastically: "Oh, you have such a hot bottom, my heart is bursting with happiness when I can caress it naked. Come on, I kiss him. I've dreamed of that for a long time," he said. And already he bent down and kissed my bottom. He grunted gleefully. But my God, what did he do then. He licked my ass with his tongue. I groaned loudly. That made him do it harder and harder. I squeezed my bum as hard as I could in his face and was totally beside myself with excitement. "Come on in now." I pleaded with him. "I can't take it anymore." Now he got up and pressed his wand into me. I felt how he was digging his member deeper and deeper into me. My whole body is trembling with delight. But even Paul didn't last long the first time and I noticed how his warm love juice filled my body. A long, loud moan came from deep within us. After Paul's member left me too, I turned around. We looked at each other and were both speechless with happiness. There was only one thing left to do. We hugged and kissed. After that, an exciting time began for us. We experienced unimaginable feelings of happiness for ourselves. And soon they used every opportunity, at every place that came up, to live out this exciting new experience as often as possible. When we have free time, we do it in my room. If someone was in the house who could have heard us, we ran into the adjacent forest. There we had built a small leaf hut in a hiding place, where we could let off steam undisturbed to our hearts' content. When I was working on the farm, Paul often helped and we kept ourselves busy in the barn whenever possible. We were undisturbed there. Then we constantly grabbed our crotch and kneaded our bumps until our beatings became hard again. After that, we always jumped on each other with enthusiasm. But only when my parents were in the field and couldn't see us. If they were in the yard, we looked for a place in the barn where the entrance was not immediately visible. Then we pulled the other's pants down while he leaned on a bale of straw and kept an eye on the entrance. The other grabbed between his legs from behind and milked him. At the same time, we could stroke and kiss our butts. Sometimes we would slide our fingers in while we continued to vigorously milk the hard, twitching club of the other. This often happened more than once a day.

In winter we took responsibility for two feeding troughs near our house. We had to be there every day to get fresh hay from the shed next to it. We were undisturbed there. After we filled them with fresh food, we ran impatiently into the hay barn and often stayed there for a long time. It was warm and cozy in there even in winter. In addition, we both found the smell of hay pleasant, which also spurred us on to give free rein to our lust. When we had once again been very wild and didn't come home until the evening, my mother looked at me a little worried at dinner and said:

"You look so pale and tired. Maybe you shouldn't work that much. " That's okay. I have a lot of fun. Just let me do it. "I then answered.

Paul fell in love with me and I loved him too. Despite my initial fantasies, I couldn't imagine how strong the feelings for him would develop. Now we were both crazy for each other and our friendship turned into a passionate love affair. But I also love Eva. After this hot summer with her, I went to Munich now and then, because I didn't want to wait for her for 11 months. When I was with her again, I asked her: "Do you have any other boys besides me?" "You mean sex?" She asked. "Yes," I answered. "You are my best friend, but I also have sex with other guys, because you are so seldom with me." She answered honestly to my question. "That's fine as long as I'm number one for you," I replied. "I've had fun with a girl before." She confessed to me. "So did you like it?" I asked. "Yes. I think I'll do that more often. " Oh, I'd like to be there! " I shouted jokingly. "I ask her." She answered. I was surprised and happy about it. "Do you have someone else besides me?" She wanted to know from me now.

"No, you know the girls from our village. There's nothing clever about it. But I have fun with my friend Paul sometimes. "I replied. "Oh, that is good. You're best friends and I'm sure you have a lot of fun together. "She knew how much I liked it when she spoiled my buttocks. It was only what gave me a taste for it. Or was it Paul? "I would like to be there too, to watch how you do it," she said then. "Let's see." I replied. Now she wanted to know everything we are up to. I told her and then asked about her experiences with her friend. She also described in detail what she experienced with her. That was interesting and exciting for me. When Eva noticed this, we interrupted our conversation and first made love.

After we lay together, satisfied and exhausted, I said to her: "I'm a little worried about Paul." "Why is he sick?" She asked a little worried. "No, but he's never had sex with a girl. Always with me He should also gain experience with a girl. " And what if he doesn't want that because he only likes boys?" She replied. "Well, then that would be okay too. But he should test it first. I like girls and I would be happy if we could share this lust with each other. "Then she was quiet for a few minutes. Which was unusual then she asked, "And why did you tell me that?" I had to smile. She knew me very well and already knew why. "Well, you said yes, you'd like to see how we do it together. How about if you take part? Then Paul can gain his first experience and maybe get a taste for it. "I looked at her with honest eyes. "I already imagined what it would be like for three people. I'm curious, yes. "She answered. "Well then we'll do it in the summer when you're there. I'll just discuss this, with Paul. I think he'll be thrilled. "I drove home the next day. This time it wasn't long before I saw Eva again. The summer vacation began in just under four weeks. Then we would meet again on the hill every day.

When I got home, Paul picked me up from the train station. It was 1.5 km from our farm when we took the shortcut through the forest. Paul was walking along a narrow path in front of me and I was looking at his hot little bottom the whole time. That excited me until I couldn't take it any longer. When the path got wider again, I ran to him with a hammer in my pants and put my hand to his bottom. "I'm so horny for you. Come on, we'll quickly escape into the bushes. "I now stroked his bottom even more passionately. Paul beamed at me and asked: "Why are we still on the way here?" We ran into the thicket and quickly took off our clothes. I turned Paul around, who immediately fell to his knees and willingly offered me his little bum. What a wonderful sight that was again. Immediately I knelt behind him and penetrated him. Paul moved his bottom back and forth, turned it a little in a circle, and exulted with happiness. So he showed me how he missed me and I was happy about it. He kept emphasizing how much he loves me. After spending the past few days with Eva, Paul's bum was a revelation to me. So it didn't take long and I poured myself into him with a loud moan. After seeing Paul in his ecstatic bliss, I was also eager to finally be ridden by him again. Eva bought an anal dildo in Munich to give me the greatest pleasure. That was awesome too, but Paul's member, on which the whole guy hung and who trembled and moaned, was unrivaled for me. Now I crouched down and lifted my bum high up. "It's your turn" I shouted. "Oh, you are beautiful," Paul exclaimed enthusiastically when he saw me in this position. Immediately he began to passionately wet my hole with his tongue. That catapulted me instantly into the highest excitement. Then he slowly pushed his member into me. I began to move too and got faster and faster. He shouted, "Not so fast, I'll be right there." But it was too late, I was so frenzied that I was no longer able to throttle it. "Come on, I want to feel it in me." I mature. A short time later I felt his member ceaselessly jumping back and forth in me while it squirted the pent-up love juice into me. And it didn't stop that quickly. He whimpered and moaned incessantly. Then he said somewhat guiltily, "I've been waiting for you for so long and I've been full of my semen. He wanted out. That couldn't be stopped. " You don't have to apologize. It was fantastic how you injected endlessly into me. Besides, as I know each other, it won't be the last time today. "And we both gripped each other.

When we got to my house, I told him that I had arranged with Eva to introduce him to sex games with a girl. "Eva makes herself available for this." I proclaimed proudly. "But you can't make a difference without asking me," he said, slightly sullen. I didn't expect him to react like that, which is why I expressed myself a bit clumsily. "No, we didn't decide, we just discussed that it would be nice for us if you would take part.

I would especially like to lie with you with a woman. We should try it out. You have never done it before. Maybe you like it too. If not, it doesn't matter. We have each other anyway and nothing will change that. "I now explained more diplomatically. Especially after the last sentence, Paul's face brightened up again. "Well, we'll try it then, but you have to explain everything to me beforehand so that I don't embarrass myself." I'll be there and help you. " Okay." At the end, he confirmed our plan in a confident voice. And because he was lying on his stomach and his adorable bottom jumped in my eye, I quickly lay down on him. "Yes, then let's seal this pact right now," I said, rubbing myself hard against him while he pushed his bottom upwards.

A month later the summer vacation began and Eva came back to the village. Since she didn't know when she was arriving this time, we agreed that she would come and see me as soon as she arrived. I sat with Paul on the bench in front of the house. We have been there for a while. The sun was shining and it charged our batteries with its warm rays. I noticed that the bulge in his pants was getting bigger again. Aha, the battery will be full in a minute, I thought. I was looking forward to it and was just about to suggest disappearing into the barn with him when I saw Eva coming down the street from afar. Immediately my plan changed. I ran towards her and we kissed passionately as we greeted her. Then we went to Paul, who was still sitting on the bench. He got up and greeted Eva. She said, "Oh, you look good. You have become a real man now. "And looked down at his bump." Yes, training with Max does that." He replied, grinning cheekily. "I can understand that very well. Max is a good trainer" she replied and grinned too. I thought this is a good start. Now all that's missing is that they rave about my hot ass together and smiled. "I hope to see you again soon," said Eva to Max. "Yes, see you soon." Eva turned to me and explained that she had to go to her grandparents first. We wanted to meet up on the hill in two hours after that.

When she was gone, Paul said: "She's cool" and his eyes beamed at me. "I've always said that," I answered dryly. "But what was that in your pants earlier. Before Eva came, there was a big bump and now there is nothing to be seen. "I said, pretending to be disappointed." Oh, you don't have to worry about that," Paul replied with a laugh. "It'll rise again by the time we're in the barn." That was a bit of an exaggeration, but when we got there, it didn't take long and I felt it inside me. Such a petite boy and always ready. Where does it get all the power from, I thought and was happy. When he had finished his hot ride in me, he left me alone, which was unusual for him. "You still need the strength for Eva," he explained to me.

"You don't have to worry your head about that. Eva doesn't miss out, and neither does you. "I said in a confident voice. He grinned at me: "Well I'll make sure that I don't miss out." And we both laughed. But still, nothing happened between us that afternoon. When I walked to the hill, I was happy about it, because I was looking forward to Eva and since we hadn't seen each other for a month, it would be a hot, long date with her. And that's how it happened.

After we had finally lived out our lust again without restraint, we lay exhausted and content on the grass.

"If you think the time is right, bring Paul with you. I'm looking forward to it. "Said, Eva. "Good, then he'll come with you tomorrow." We said goodbye. "I love you, Max." "I love you too, Eva." We kissed goodbye and ran home. On the way there, I looked up Paul at home and asked him if he would like to come with me the next day. "Yes, I'm looking forward to it." He replied. I was happy about it, but it still looked weird. So I replied: "Paul, why do you say that. I can see that something is wrong with you." I feel quite uncomfortable. This is the first time and now on command. But I won't pinch and come with you tomorrow. "He said. I thought everything will be fine and I was looking forward to the next day as well.

The next day was Sunday. Although the cattle also had to be looked after on the farm, I was mostly released from work that day. That means we had Sunday all to ourselves. We had an appointment with Eva right afternoon. I picked Paul up from home and we walked up the hill together for the first time. Eva had not yet arrived. So we sat down on the grass and looked at the mountains and enjoyed this wonderful sight for a while, which Paul was not yet familiar with. Every corner of the small town was familiar to us. We grew up here and also knew the neighboring forests. We felt connected and secure in this piece of home. I felt a sense of joy and gratitude to be able to live here with my friend. But at some point we got bored. We had been waiting for Eva for half an hour. "If she doesn't come yet, we could warm up a bit," I said. Paul looked at me smiling and we kissed. Not long, then we were lying on the grass. Suddenly I heard Eva say amusingly from behind: "As I can see, you have already started without me." "If you let me wait that long. Besides, we haven't started yet. That looks different. "I replied with a smile, too.

We sat down again and Paul moved a little away from me and showed Eva with an inviting movement that she should also sit down with us. "Oh thank you. It's an honor to sit between two such handsome boys, "she said coquettishly. She took her offered seat, looked at Paul, and asked: "Have you no experience with girls at all?" He replied: "Not really." "Have you kissed one before?" "No, just Max." "Yes, Max is good at kissing. But let's try it out with each other. "Then she kissed him. Paul immediately showed full commitment and immediately became very passionate about it. "Don't stop so wild. We, women, want to take it a little slower. Kiss me more tenderly. "And he did while I watched them. After a while, Eva turned her head to me and kissed me too. I laid her on the grass while kissing and slowly let my hand slide up her crotch. When I got to the top and I gently caressed her labia, she moaned softly. I took off her panties and slipped my fingers through her crevice until her clit emerged. Then I played with it and she tipped her head back with a moan.

Now I turned to Paul, who was watching with interest. I kissed him while I continued rubbing Eva's clitoris. "Come on, try it," I whispered to him. Paul put his hand in her crotch. "Do you see that clitoris there?" He nodded. "Put your finger through her crevice and then rub it." When he had started, Eva was excited again. "Now faster." He obeyed and Eva groaned louder. "Even faster than, as fast as you can," I told him. Eva was now tossing her whole upper body back and forth in excitement. When Paul saw this he was excited too, and he tried to get everything right. I watched his member slowly straighten up until he had reached his full size and was very happy about it. "Keep it up, I'll take off your pants and me while you continue to bring Eva into ecstasy," I whispered to him. When I had undressed her, I said to him: "Now kneel between her legs and go with your tongue through her crevice." When he noticed how wild Eva was getting, he didn't stop. He was on his knees with his head bowed down.

I saw the adorable little bum that was standing high in the air. Now you should feel the same happiness as Eva, I thought and kissed his hot bottom, which was already wide open in this position. Running my tongue through his furrow and then massaged his hole with it. He moaned hard, stretched his bum higher, and sunk his head even deeper into Eva's lap. They shouted: "Oh yes Paul, that's great. Keep it up. "Which further encouraged him. And I did the same with him. Paul and Eva were now completely turned away. After a while, I lay on my back, pushed my head under his stomach, and took his hard member in my mouth while I ran two fingers into him from behind and massaged his prostate incessantly. With my tongue, I licked the glans vigorously, which jumped back and forth with excitement, while his hard member pumped vigorously. He couldn't stand it for long and came with a roar. Eva had calmed down in the meantime, which told me that she had also had an orgasm. But knowing her, she was soon ready for a new game. Paul turned to one side and lay on the grass while I continued to occupy myself with Eva.

 "Come on all fours in front of me," I said to her. "I'll take you from behind." She quickly took this position and I slowly pushed my member into her. Always in and out. She groaned loudly and shouted, "Yes, that's crazy. Don't stop there anytime soon. I'm so hot. "Paul watched with wide eyes. After a while, I asked him: "Come on, stand in front of me." He stood with his legs apart over Eva, turned to me and I began to suck his flaccid penis. While Eva moved her body back and forth and so rode on my member, I had Paul's penis in my mouth and licked it wildly with my tongue. Not long and I felt how it got bigger and bigger again. That was an exciting and pleasurable experience for me. When the time had come and his member was back in all its glory in front of my face, I said to him: "Now go back and inside me." He looked at me enthusiastically: "Really?" He asked. "Yes, but hurry up, Eva ride my member like crazy. I can't take it long before it comes to me. "He quickly knelt behind me and soon I felt him inside me. At the same time, Eva was riding on my member and I finally lost control. "Yes, yes, faster, faster." I mature and both of them got even wilder in and around me. I was between them and didn't move. I let this unique hot ride go through me, rattled it, and turned my upper body in excitement. Then it came to me with all my might. Since both continued like better, I couldn't get away from them so quickly. Finally, I said to Paul: "Get him out of me and stick him in with Eva." I left Eva and he slipped into her excitedly. "Oh, you are amazing," she exclaimed. And kept moving. Now on Paul his member.

After recovering for a few minutes, I watched them both. For Paul, it was the second time in a short time. It looked super awesome to see Eva moving ecstatically and moaning while Paul was inside of her. He had his mouth slightly open and his eyes closed.

He was breathing heavily. He didn't leave Eva alone with her movements for long, but found the right rhythm with her and moved his pelvis to and fro. Both had their mouths open wide now and were moaning lustfully together. I saw Paul's bum again, driving back and forth, and regretted not having an erection. I would have loved to drive into him now while he was in Eva. Paul looked at me briefly and as if he could read my mind, he said: "Come on now and stand in front of me." I stood in front of him with my legs apart. He took my limp member completely in his mouth. He worked it hard with his tongue. He had practice at it and was damn good at it. It wasn't the first time he'd got me going again. This time he became particularly passionate about it. He probably wanted me to penetrate him too while he was in Eva. I closed my eyes and imagined. I knew him. Surely then he would freak out. It then succeeded through his tireless stimulation of my member and my imagination. It got stiff again. I didn't want to waste a second and immediately knelt behind him. In this position he tried, as far as he could, to open his furrow for me. When I slowly penetrated him, he called out: "Oh yes." Now he turns completely off. He moved his body like a madman, grunting and whimpering. Even in my imagination, I couldn't imagine it that way. It was overwhelming how he stood between me and Eva, trembling and gasping with ecstasy. Then it soon came to him. He was shaking all over and it didn't stop that quickly. Then Eva called: "I can no longer. I'm exhausted. "Paul took his member out of her and she lay down on the grass, completely exhausted. Then she cried. We bent over her, still exhausted, and stroked her. "What's my love?" I asked. "It's just your nerves. It was so overwhelming. " You were wonderful Eva, ,,Paul said and I confirmed it to her too. All three of us were happy and satisfied that day. After that, the three of us always met on the hill. And when we sometimes took Eva in the middle and penetrated her from the front and back at the same time, she was finally overwhelmed by both of us.

Two weeks later Paul asked me: "I am always there now. Don't you want to be alone with Eva again? "The question surprised me." Why, don't you like it anymore?" I asked. "Very much. But in between, we both have fun together, without Eva. "He gave as the reason for his question. "I've been alone with Eva the whole time and I'll be back when I go to Munich to see her. But you've never been with a girl without me Do you want to be alone with her sometime? "I offered him. "No, she is your friend. I don't want that. I'd rather find another girl for that. " Here in our village?" I asked mockingly. "Yes, why not. The girls here also have needs and feelings, there is sure to be someone who likes to take part. "He said a little defiantly." You're right," I replied guiltily, then just like I said it was arrogant and pretty wrong. Maybe I was a little jealous because he wanted to be with another girl.

So I said to him, "When you've found one, the four of us will go up the hill. You can crumble with her later if you want to be alone with her. The place is big enough. Will you come to Eva with me until then? "I asked him, a little unsettled." Yes, of course, if you and Eva want it." I looked him in the eye and said: "Of course we want that. I love you, Paul." Paul beamed at me, kissed me, and then didn't let go of me so quickly.

"This is the first time you've told me that. I love you too, Max, with all my heart. "

After four days Paul found a girl or woman who came up with him on the hill. Her name was Maria and she was twelve years older than us. She looked pretty for her age. Maria already had a lot of experience and was known for it in the village. A good choice for Paul, I thought. The four of us sat on the hill for a while and talked. Maria lived alone and had a small tailor shop in town. However, since her income was insufficient for the few customers, she also sewed for a larger company working from home. She also had a small farm, which she mainly used for self-sufficiency. She was very hardworking and we admired her for it. In the village, she was a little notorious for her male acquaintances. They often visited her. The men were mostly from outside, which aroused suspicion in such a village. Some, therefore, claim that she works as a prostitute on the side. The longer I looked at Maria, the prettier I found her. She had a slim figure, long black hair, and a large chest that I had to stare at all the time. Finally, however, Eva wanted to cuddle with me now and kissed me. Paul turned to Maria and kissed her too. I put Eva on the grass and we hugged tightly. Paul said to his new companion: "Come on, let's go a bit." "But we can stay here too," she replied. "No, I want to be alone with you." Took her hand and stood up with her.

A few meters further they found a place to sit down on. They couldn't be seen and Eva then occupied all of my attention. After a while, we were lying next to each other, exhausted. Now we heard the other two groans. I smiled and said, "That seems to be working." And then came a deep roar. I was already very familiar with that. "Now he's hosed down," I said to Eva, laughing softly. "I know that too." She answered because she had heard it often enough. We waited for them to emerge from their love nest with us. But the two didn't come. After a short while, we heard Maria again. She started moaning again, getting louder and louder ... I knew Paul was a boisterous man and his best piece too. He was having a lot of fun. I thought that was great. "I think it will take a while, with both of them," I said. "Do you want to play a new game?" My grandma is waiting for me today. I promised her I would help her cook the fruit. "Said Eva, getting dressed. At that moment Paul and Maria came out from behind the bushes. Her hair was messed up and they both looked very pleased. I looked at Paul questioningly and he grinned back cheekily. Then we talked briefly and he invited Maria over for the next day. Tomorrow again? He's not exaggerating now, I thought. But Maria agreed.

Then I ran home with him. On the way there I was bursting with curiosity: "How was it?" I wanted to know. "Quite good." He said nothing more about it. "Did you do a lot with Eva today?" He asked me then.

And since he hadn't given me an exhaustive answer myself, I said briefly: "Yes." "I ask because I wanted to know if you're still interested today. I would like to feel you inside me again and pamper you again. "Since when have you been asking me if I feel like it? Did I ever say no? "I looked at him with a grin. Then we quickly went straight to the barn. After we had let off steam, he told me in detail what he had experienced with Maria. I asked him: "Why did you invite her over again for tomorrow? Don't you want to be with me and Eva anymore? " Yes," he said. "If it's okay with you, I'll stay with you tomorrow. Let's see what happens there. " But Maria is from our place. When she sees that the two of us are having sex, the whole place will soon know about it. That means we can't have fun together then. " I didn't even think about that. This is crap. Then tomorrow it will be the last time that she will be there. "

The next morning, my father came to me and said, "Today we have to go out to the field and bring the feed into the barn. A thunderstorm is supposed to come in the evening. If the food gets wet again, it will spoil us. " Well then I'll run to Paul and let them know that I don't have time today." I called and ran to him. But Paul was immediately ready to help me and wanted to come with me. "But who will let the girls know?" I asked. "They'll notice that we're not coming. Then they are just among themselves. Girls like that now and then anyway. "I smiled because I knew Eva's fantasies. Nevertheless, I called her and let her know. Since Maria didn't pick up her phone and the answering machine didn't start either, I couldn't leave her a message. So Eva wanted to run to the hill at the appointed time and meet her. "Good," I said. "Then I wish you both a lot of fun." Then we drove to the field with my father to bring the feed into the barn. With Paul's help, we were finished sooner than planned. My father then drove the trailer to the neighbor. He too was fetching the hay from the field. He wanted to help him. During this time we stowed our hay in the barn. When we finished our work, we were satisfied with our work. "What do we do now? Do we want to go up the hill to the girls? "I asked because it wasn't that late yet. Paul grinned at me cheekily and said: "Do you want that?" The scent of fresh hay filled the barn and erotic feelings broke out in us again. When I noticed the bulge in Paul's pants, which had already grown considerably larger, I ran to him and took his hand. His hand was already very hot. This heat carried over to me too. I could feel the warmth of his hand transfer to mine and then climb up the arm. Until it gradually ran like a wave through my whole body. Oh, how wonderful it was again when it got hot between my loins and my love pin began to twitch. So I quickly pulled him behind the bales of straw that were piled up in a corner of the barn. Then we quickly took off our clothes and fell madly upon ourselves. We enjoyed being to ourselves again. As always, we couldn't get enough of each other. It was only in the evening when my mother called us for dinner that we came out of our hiding place completely exhausted. Paul stayed to eat, of course. When we entered the kitchen, pale and sweaty, my mother looked at us in shock. "How do you look? Sit down quickly guys, eat and drink properly first. You are exhausted. "She said and put bowls with food on the table. Paul replied: "Thank you, but it was nice that we could let off steam again." "Yes, it was." I quickly confirmed. "Well, I'm glad that I have two such strong men who can tackle things in the courtyard." She said at the end. Then she ran back into the stable to feed the cattle.

We gripped each other and began to fill our bellies because after this action we were very hungry. I said playfully caring: "Paul is eating properly. You deserved it today. "I shifted my bottom noticeably back and forth on the chair and grinned at him." Then you hit it because you were at least as hard-working." He replied. I calculated in my mind what had happened in the barn behind the straw. Then I said a little proud: "That's right. I'm even a point in the lead. "Because I had squirted out my love juice once more than he did. Paul protested: "But you also have to include the time in your bill." I let the afternoon go through my head with him in the straw. Suddenly my pride evaporated because I realized that he was lying in front of me with a few points. Paul just had more stamina than me. I said quickly in a confident voice: "Well, then undecided." He smiled and replied: "Yes, made a difference. But that doesn't matter, the main thing is that we were both happy. And I was as happy as I haven't been for a long time. "I looked at him with beaming eyes, nodded in agreement, and said fervently: "Me too."

The next day we met again on the hill. When Paul and I arrived, Eva was already there. We sat down next to her on the grass and waited for Maria. In the meantime I asked her, "So how was it yesterday? Did you have a nice afternoon together? ". She smiled and nodded vigorously. I laughed: "Well then it worked." Paul looked at us questioningly. "Maria and Eva had a hot girl afternoon yesterday," I explained to him. He still hadn't got it right. "Does that mean you had sex with each other?" And looked at Eva in disbelief. "Yes," she replied briefly. Now Paul was completely off his socks. "That's awesome. Do you do it again today? I would like to take a look. " Who are you telling me that." I shoved after confirming. Immediately afterward Maria came. When she said our beaming faces, she looked at Eva questioningly. "I told the boys about yesterday." Eva said to her.

Maria looked at us: "You two also jump more often."

"How did you get that?" I asked her. "Well, you always look so happy. No boy your age looks like this if he doesn't have a balanced sex life. And since you both look so happy together, the question arises where you live out your instincts, if not together. "When we were silent, she continued:" Sorry, I didn't want to embarrass you. I don't care if you are gay, bi, or straight. The main thing is that you are happy. I think it's great how you do it. Unlike some of the people here in town, whom I know secretly get on with each other. Whether with another woman or a man or with both. There is everything here too. But officially they rail against it. You're doing it right. The main thing is that you are happy. You have my appreciation for that. There is no way I will talk to anyone else about it. So let's just be happy together. " You are right." Paul said and kissed me in front of her eyes. She smiled at us: "You look really cute doing it. That fits. Please more of it. " Then we want to see how you enjoy your" I replied.

Then she kissed Eva and they began to caress. First gently on the neck and then each other's breasts. Slowly they got going and took off their blouses. They weren't wearing a bra. Maria's breasts were very large and firm. Her nipples looked huge from it and her nipples were already quite stiff and stood in the middle of the hill. Eva noticed this too and played with admiration at it. Then she suckled on them. That aroused Marie instantly "Oh how I love that." She exclaimed. "Yes, that always makes her horny, once it's your turn, she becomes completely uninhibited and you can do whatever you want with her," Paul whispered to me softly. "And where do I have to go to your place so that you surrender to me unrestrainedly?" I asked him. "You know that. You can always do what you want with me. "And smiled at me sweaty. That was enough for me.

I grabbed him and we kissed. Then we quickly undressed and when he was under me, I lifted his legs and pushed them forward so that his bottom opened wide and came up. Then I penetrated him. "I love you." He whispered excitedly. When we heard the two girls moaning and they kept crying lustfully, moaning: "Yes, yes, go on!" We too finally lost our temper. We united front and back, sometimes him and then me. We also formed a noisy backdrop. After an hour we were exhausted.

Now we looked at the two girls. They were also lying contentedly on the grass and had their eyes closed.

I looked at Maria's big nipples. "What do you think if she's still going to be mindless when we suck on her nipples?" I asked Paul. "I don't know, but I think so," he replied. We crawled to her quietly. One from the left and the other from the right. At the same time, we sucked hard on her nipples. Maria was startled and groaned loudly. She wanted to push away. But the harder she tried to get away, the harder we sucked on her already hard nipples. Finally, she surrendered and moaned loudly. "Yes, yes, you make me so horny." She cried. In doing so, she opened her legs and fasted herself into the crotch. When Eva saw this, she too was awake again. She pushed her hand away from Maria and put her face between her thighs. Marie was now completely beside herself. She started sweating and whimpering. Then she grabbed us with her hands and wanted to get between our legs. So we knelt but always stuck to her nipples, which we had already sucked on. In this position, Maria easily reached our pleasure syringes, which quickly straightened up again, and ran her hands along with them violently. She turned our stiff limbs slightly in all directions and at the same time gently played with her thumb on the acorns. Oh, she knew how to ecstasy a man. Eva looked up briefly and noticed our butts as they stood up within reach of her arms. As she sank her head back into Maria's crotch, she stretched out her arms and stuck a finger into each of us, shaking them violently inside us. In and then always a little back and forth. She massaged our prostate. She was also a professional at it and catapulted us into an indescribable ecstasy. Meanwhile, Marie slid along our limbs, which were already twitching with excitement, and we pulled her nipples powerfully with our mouths. We wanted to get Marie out of control just for fun, but now the girls had us, in the truest sense of the word, firmly under their control. Paul and I had risen to the peak of lust and it came to us almost at the same time. A short time later, Maria lifted her pelvis and groaned loudly. It also got an unmistakable climax. Then she fell exhausted on the grass. We let go of her and looked into her face. She opened her eyes, smiled, and said: "You are devils but love." We grudged at her and replied: "But you too." I turned to Eva and said: "And you are the worst." I! "she exclaimed, played outraged with her innocent expression.

Mary explained to us that day that in the future she would no longer be able to come to us on the hill. She had a small yard and a lot of work. "You can visit me," she offered us. When she was gone we talked about it. But Eva didn't feel like doing it.

"I wanted to be with a woman again. That was very nice, but now I've satisfied my lust for a while. "I had Eva and Paul myself, so I didn't think further meetings were important. Only Paul decided to visit her.

After he had visited Maria for the second time, he came to me late in the evening and said with a serious face: "Max, we have to talk to each other." "What's going on?" "Come on, let's go out and run a little." He asked me. It was already dark and we were walking out of the village on this extraordinary warm summer evening along a small dirt road. Paul had four bottles of beer in his backpack. The look on his face told me that something important was on his mind. At the edge of a cornfield, we sat down in the gas and drank beer.

Finally, he started to say: "Max, you are the most important person in my life. Nobody has ever been so important to me. I love you and I want to be and stay with you. I don't like it when I go to Maria and you're not there, at least not around. I know you might think it's stupid, but that's how I feel. I would like to have women with you too. I think that's nice but only with you. What do you think if we both stay together and later start an extended family? I would also like to have children one day. Let's look for women who suit us. We saw that they exist. Eva and Maria would be suitable partners for this. But Marie already has her own life and Eva will probably never move in with us. But we now know that there are these girls or women who suit us. Please let's try. "

I answered him. "Paul, I don't think it's stupid that you want to be around me, even when you're with a woman. Because that's how I feel when you're not around. I'm missing something without you. I can be alone on the hill with Eva. But only because you've been there many times. You are somehow close to me anyway, even when you are not there. And I know that Eva became very fond of you too. I even believe that she misses you when I come to her alone. You are also the most important person in my life and I cannot imagine being without you. We'll find a way together. And if Eva doesn't come to us in the village, which I strongly believe, we will eventually get to know two other girls. We can then father children with them because I want that too. "

After I had committed to our friendship, I smiled and joked afterward: "Your horny little bottom is the center of my life and excites me to the utmost." And already I thought of caressing and kissing him again. But the thought always comes before the action. Before I was able to implement it, Paul shouted indignantly: "Stop it, Max! With such a serious subject, my bum isn't the most important thing. "I laughed and continued:" But if it is. Perhaps it is not the most important thing, but the most beautiful thing, or do you not like my bottom that much? "I asked, pretending to be insecure. "Of course he excites me as well. Nothing is hotter than your firm bottom, but ... "You see!" I interrupted him. "We even agree on that." And smacked him. "You are impossible Max." He said and then smiled too. Then he came and kissed me. "Everything has been said. Let's show how much we love each other. "I said to him. A short time later we were lying naked on the grass. Paul lay on his stomach and lifted his bottom, which for me that night shone like the planet of the little prince in the moonlight. The only thing missing was the flower, and I thought of my favorite book "The Little Prince". But since he had just rebuked me, I did nothing and didn't say a word about it. That was not usually my style. So he asked me: "Is what you just said is true, is he the center of your life?" He wiggled his bottom slightly. "Oh yes," I said enthusiastically as I looked at him and my heart was beating faster. I pick a poppy that was standing next to me in the grass and put it in his bottom. "Now it's perfect," I summed up delightedly and then kissed all parts of this little miracle that sparkled in the moonlight, which he was now stretching higher towards me. We fell into an unrestrained and wild ecstasy. Never before have had we so often affirmed our love for one another. It was only when it was light that we ended the passionate hugs, but only because we feared that we would be spotted in the cornfield.

We decided that we would first meet again with Eva on the hill. She would be happy about it too, I was sure of that. When the vacation was slowly coming to an end, she drove back to Munich. We said goodbye to her at the train station. On the way home I thought, although I love Paul and at this moment I can't imagine anything better than a future together with him, I was at the same time crazy about the wild and unrestrained games with Eva. And not only that. She was my best friend and I loved her too. I still found it normal and was extremely happy with it. At the same time, I was eyeing Paul's tight little bottom again, who was walking along the narrow forest path in front of me.

Drawing folder "Der Liebesreigen"
-Miniature excerpt 3-

3. Girl fantasies

"Boys are all stupid," Susi said when she greeted me when she stormed excitedly into my apartment. She stood in the hallway, completely distraught. I ran to her and hugged her. "First sit down and calm down," I said and accompanied her to my room. We were best friends and she had a date with the most desirable boy in class today. Then she came to me straight away to tell me how it was and what happened. She was pretty upset. So I asked her: "Why are you so excited?" And she started to report.

"You know that I had an appointment with Erik at the cinema today. We went to the movie yesterday that I chose. Arrived in the cinema, Erik headed straight for the back rows. The last two were already occupied. So we sat down in the next one. I would have preferred to sit further upfront, but I didn't want to complain right from the start. During the film, he put his hand on my thighs and slowly and inconspicuously led them a little higher. When he was almost at my crotch, I took his hand and held it. Since he noticed that he couldn't get any further with me, he took it away again and put his arm around my shoulder. I found that pleasant. But he kept stroking my neck with his fingers, which distracted me from the film. Behind us, couples kissed, and right next to me a boy was constantly fondling his companion. Whereby he kept whispering: "Not here, stop it." His voice sounded more like that his friend should go on after all.

I would have better told Erik that I would rather sit further ahead. But then I went back with him without protest, so he probably assumed that I was okay with his fiddling. This is what these places were known for. I thought, and a little annoyed about my inconsistency. Then he turned to me and tried to kiss me. When I turned away, he said: Come on, Suzy doesn't have you like that. Everyone here is doing this. So I gave in and we kissed. He was good at that. I wanted to kiss him that evening, but the first time he, I had imagined it differently. More romantic and not on a seat in the cinema just because everyone here is doing that. That's why I wasn't so enthusiastic about it, especially since he tried again to slide his hand between my legs. Behind me, a girl moaned softly and I turned to her briefly to see what was going on. Then I saw how her companion had his hand under her dress and was busy working under it. She had her eyes closed and was moaning softly. The two boys next to me had suddenly become very calm. I saw them put their hands on each other's large bumps in their pants. They kept scratching at it with their fingers. They couldn't see anything of the film, then their eyes were closed and their mouths slightly open. It looked cute. And I admit, it excited me a little too to see her big bumps jerky between her legs. But did it have to be in the cinema of all places? "

"Well." I said, "They may not have planned that either. But how did it go with you and Erik? "

"When the film was over, Erik suggested we stroll through the park with me. It was already dark but the air was pleasantly warm. Now comes the romantic part, I thought. He took my hand and I ran with him to the park. On the way, he kept telling me about his cycling. He was a good racing driver, but I didn't care that much about his sport to hear about it all the time. Why didn't he play an instrument, then we could talk about music, I thought. But then maybe he wouldn't have such a nice ass, and I smiled at the thought. Finally, we got to the park and he kissed me again. He pressed his body tight to mine. I felt something moving in his pants and he was getting more and more excited. I found that exciting. He took me by the hand again and led me to wake me up from the path, purposefully to a small hidden meadow. He knew his way around here. Then he sat down on the grass. Come sit with me He asked me. I didn't feel comfortable with it, but what should I do? Turn around and run home that was too stupid for me. I was interested in getting to know him. So I sat down next to him and he kissed me again. I liked that. Then suddenly he laid me on the grass and crawled on top of me. It all happened too quickly for me. He tried to open my legs, but I was strong enough to stop him. I managed to crawl out from under him and I ran away.

" Then he tried to rape you!" I exclaimed in horror. "It wasn't like that either. He let me involuntarily when he realized that I don't want to. After I crawled out from under him, he asked me to stay there. He would be sensible, he promised me. But I didn't feel like it anymore. "

When she finished with her report, I got up, got a glass of wine, and said, "Now you're here. First, take a sip and calm down. " Can I sleep with you today?" She asked me. "I don't feel like going home anymore and I don't want to be alone." It wasn't the first time that she stayed with me or me with her. "Of course you can stay here." I said. I then brought the rest of the bottle of wine that I had just opened into my room and we sit comfortably on the sofa. After the third glass, the experience with Erik was a thing of the past and we talked again about our favorite topic "boys". Suddenly Susi said: "Evelyn, I think boys don't even know what girls really want." "I already realized that." I answer. "But what means exactly?" "I mean how they behave during sex. They always strive for one thing and that as quickly as possible. When you have hosed down, it's quiet for now. Most of the time they get dressed again and say goodbye because they still have a date with their friends. "She explained to me. "Boys are too. You can't do that either. "I said somewhat resignedly. "How would sex have to look like for you to be really happy?" I then asked her. "Well without a goal. Just be tender. Without always having to think that the guy wants to stick his member inside you or that you should make him cum in some other way. It excites me when you stroke my nipples and then suck on them. If you run your finger gently and for a long time between my labia so that they swell and it becomes damp. I would then like to be licked and rubbed on the clitoris until it totally arouses me, so that I can hardly stand it" I listened to her descriptions with interest and it excites me. Since I wasn't wearing a bra and only a tight T-shirt, my hardened nipples were visible on it. When Susi saw this, she took her hands and caressed my nipples. You have nice, big nipples, she said. I started to moan softly. "Do you want me to stop?" She asked me. "If you like it, keep caressing me." I answered quietly and already a bit excited. She was circling my nipples with her palms now. Then she took them both between thumb and forefinger and turned them slightly back and forth. I moaned louder "Oh, that's wonderful," I said. We sat next to each other and I saw her dreamy look as she spoiled me in this wonderful way. Now she kissed me tenderly and put a hand on my neck. I began to stroke her breasts too. Our kisses became more passionate over time. Then she took off my shirt. She kissed my nipples and pulled them with her lips. I moaned softly and my body trembled with excitement. A little later I took them off too and we went to bed. There we kissed for a long time and played each other on our nipples. When she kissed them repeatedly with her mouth and sucked on them, she didn't come back up but slid further down. Kissed my stomach and then put her face between my legs. I allowed everything because she had already totally aroused me. With her tongue, she drove through my vagina and as she penetrated me faster and deeper, I turned completely off. I felt like I was in another world. I had never seen anything like it before. Then she stopped and I bent my pelvis upwards and groaned excitedly: "Go on. Please. "Now there was no stopping it. I was already very wet. She licked me faster and deeper with her tongue. I moaned loudly and moved my body back and forth with lust. Then it came over me. A tremendous orgasm never before experienced. I was so happy and satisfied afterward that I would never have thought possible before. Susi came back upstairs and whispered: "You are magical in your lust." Now I turned her onto her back and started the same game with her. "You should now also float in the seventh heaven." I said to her. Susi was ready and enjoyed it to the full. She opened her legs and lifted her pelvis high, circling with it while I penetrated her as deeply as I could with my vibrating tongue. Then it came to her and she fell back satisfied and happy on the bed. We were now hugging each other and after a while, we fell asleep. It was wonderful and we did it more often after that evening, with a lot of imagination and perseverance. It used to be interesting with boys too, but then they were primarily just looking for their satisfaction. In most cases, I did not get an orgasm. It was different with Susi. When we were together, her goal was to make me orgasm. And then I did the same with her. We discovered more and more ways in which we can live out our lust as women. It was relaxed and we always got our money's worth. As often and as long as we wanted.

Two months later I was at a protest for more environmental protection. Susi was unable to attend that day and therefore not there. She drove with her mother to see her aunt over the weekend. But since this event was important to me, I attended it alone. At the demo, Luca walked next to me. He came from our parallel class. I had never really noticed him before. An inconspicuous guy who didn't speak much. Someone who always wore the same clothes, a blue 501 Levis and a blue or black simple t-shirt. I never saw him in discos. But today on the protest march, his face beamed with enthusiasm. Now that we walked the demo together, I was looking at it for the first time. Luca was a handsome boy. He had a sporty figure and a firm bottom in his jeans. He was slim and had black short hair. Why I have never noticed it before, I thought. Suddenly he looked at me with his dark brown eyes and said: "This is great here, don't you think so?" "Yes, great," I answered. He took my answer as an opportunity to ask me further questions. I noticed how he tried to get into conversation with me. This boy was different from the others, which fascinated me and I allowed his curious contact. We talked animatedly during the march. After the demonstration was coming to an end, he asked me: "Would you like to have an ice cream together." It was warm and after the march, we had just completed I thought it was a good idea. So we ran to the Italian ice cream parlor, which was just nearby. But it was full. "It wasn't just us who got the idea after the march," I said to him. So he just bought us ice cream in a paper cup and we sat on a bench in the nearby park.

It was much nicer here than there. We were alone and could continue to talk undisturbed. I was starting to like being with Luca, and I was glad that he had invited me for ice cream. Luca confessed to me: "I noticed you for a long time, but I didn't know that you are so committed to protecting the environment."

"Why did you notice me?" I asked. Luca laughed: "I wanted to talk to you about environmental protection." I'm a girl and curious. "I replied flirtatiously back." Yes, sorry. I don't have that much experience with girls. I wanted to say that you are very pretty, have a great figure and beautiful breasts. " Stop, stop, you don't have to tell me that exactly. It's enough if you think I'm pretty. "I said with a smile." Okay, I think you are pretty." He corrected the statement he had just made and smiled at me with his white teeth that peek out from behind thick, sensual lips. The boy is really pretty, I thought and gave him a peck on the mouth for that smile. He blushed. "You actually have no experience with girls. If you smile at her so adorable, then you have to expect to get a kiss. "I said.

"Yes, that's right, I don't have a license. But I notice that you know your way around better. Maybe you can teach me some things about how to behave with a girl. I am a docile student," he replied. Not badly parried, I thought. He's not stupid.

"OK. If you want to get to know a girl better, invite her to the cinema or just to a museum or castle tour. " And how do I know what she likes?" If you invite her to the cinema and she doesn't feel like it but also wants to get to know you, then she will say, cinema is not good but we could… go. "I explained to him." Would you like to visit the museum with me?" He asked me now. "No, I was only recently in the museum. But you could come to me tomorrow afternoon. My parents won't be there for the weekend. I'll cook something for us as an act of revenge for your invitation to the ice cream. "I replied. He beamed at me and was happy to say yes. "How did you like the first lesson?" I asked him. "That was fantastic," he replied. Looked at me again with his irresistible smile and kissed me on the mouth. "Oh, I can tell you learned quickly," I said pretended to be self-important. "Yes." He replied, "And I'm looking forward to tomorrow's lesson. Unfortunately, I have to leave you now. I have an important appointment with my parents. "He stood up. I stayed seated on the bench and was at eye level with the bulge that was visible on his pants between his crotches. So either our conversation has aroused him so much that his penis swelled up or he has a huge hammer in his pants, I thought. We said goodbye with a kiss. He had to lean down on me because I stayed seated. After all, I liked the view. When he turned around, I examined his firm bottom, which I had already noticed during the demonstration. At eye level, I saw him move as he walked away. My assessment was extremely positive.

Why does this horny guy have no experience with girls yet? I wondered. Maybe he's gay. Only then would he not have had to run down on me. I found that I knew too little about him to answer that question today. So I wanted to wait for the next day when he came to me and see how things develop between us.

I spent the entire Saturday morning preparing food for Luca and me. I was a little excited, but the work distracted me from it. That's why I started doing it early. I conjured up my mixed salad, which I was famous for in our family, and prepared a homemade pizza. I bought the dough ready-made, but the tomato sauce and topping were my creations. I had cheese. Salami, mushrooms, peppers, and ham cut to size. When Luca came, he should tell me what he would like on his pizza.

Exactly at 5:00 p.m. he stood at the door and rang the doorbell. I opened the door for him and asked him to come in. He had brought a bottle of red wine which he held out to me in the hallway. "I hope it goes with the meal," he said. "Yes, there is pizza," I answered.

"Oh, you couldn't have done better. It's my absolute favorite food. "We'd forgotten to greet each other out of sheer excitement. So I said to him: "So welcome then." And we kissed each other. "When can you kiss a girl properly?" He asked with his irresistible smile. "That is different. The best thing to do is just try it out. "And then we kissed for the first time. And when we looked each other in the eye afterward and they revealed brightly: "I want more." We kissed for the second time, this time longer and more passionately. After a while, I broke up with him. "Come on, choose what you want on the pizza." I took Luca by the hand and led him into the kitchen. There I showed him the prepared ingredients. When he had examined the possibilities that were there for the pizza topping, he said "everything" and laughed. "Well, I'll put it on top right away and put it in the oven. It takes about 30 minutes for the oven to get hot and baked. "I started to top the pizza and he helped me with it. In between

I opened the bottle of wine he had brought and we drank a glass while preparing the meal. The red wine was lovely and to my liking. Since I hadn't eaten anything, I was already feeling the effects of the alcohol and I was loosening up. I noticed how Luca was watching me when I walked through the kitchen and I also looked at him more often. Again and again, I looked at the large bump in his pants, which I had noticed the first time.

It crackled between us, but we held back. We talked about the demonstration we were at and then talked about our interests. He was in a swimming club. No wonder he has such a hot ass, I thought. I told him about my yoga class. He was also interested in what I noticed about it from his questions. When the pizza was ready, we set the table in the living room. We sat down and ate, drank, and chatted with one another. I felt comfortable with him and had the feeling that we had known each other for a long time. When we had finished eating and had set the table together, we sat in the living room with the third glass of wine. "And what does your second lesson look like now?" He asked, looking at me with bright eyes. "Before I can start with the next lesson, I have to find out something about your previous knowledge." "My previous knowledge is purely theoretical," he said. Really? I asked. "Yes." "With the girls and the boys?" My question aimed to determine whether he wasn't a little gay after all. He laughed and replied: "Let's leave the curious boy games aside. With girls, there is only theoretical knowledge. "Then we kissed again. "Shall I show you how you can make her happy?" "Oh, that's more than I hoped for, but of course with great pleasure." After the third glass of the sweet, heavy wine, I was brave and said: „Then take off your clothes. „Did I say that now? I wondered. He looked at me with wide eyes: "Really?" I realized that I had been a little too brash. What I attributed to alcohol. But now I couldn't back down, otherwise, I would have lost my credibility. Therefore, a little more cautiously, I confirmed my request again: "Yes, but only if you want. I don't want to make you do it. "I answered. Slowly and somewhat uncertainly, he took off his shirt.

Despite his youth, he had a broad chest and muscular arms as a result of the sport he played. There were only a few tiny plum hairs on his chest. Then he unbuttoned his pants and looked at me: "And you?" He asked. "Later. You can better watch me. "He was satisfied with the answer. He took off his pants and finally the boxer shorts. Now he stood naked in front of me in all its glory. My mouth opened in amazement and stayed in that position for a while. He already had an erection and a huge member was standing vertically on his stomach. It got damp in my crotch when I saw this wonderful boy naked in front of me and had to pull myself together not to go straight into the full program with him. "Well, you." He said. Now I undressed and he was watching me. At the same time, his member jumped excitedly. I was so torn that after I had finished undressing, I ran over to him and we kissed.

His huge penis lay on my book and exuded a great deal of warmth. He was moaning softly. I didn't want him to have an orgasm that quickly. This horny boy should inspire my imagination with his excitement for as long as possible. So I broke away from him and said, "I'll tell you now what I like most and you tell me what turns you on as we get closer." "Yes." He whispered excitedly. To calm him down a bit, I stood behind him, led my arms forward, and gently caressed his chest and stomach, then his back, until I reached his beautiful bottom and ran my hand between his buttocks. He groaned again. "Do you like that?" I asked. "Yes." He breathed. "You should say if you like it without my having to ask you." And gave him a pat on the bottom. "That excites me even more." He exclaimed. So I slapped his ass again. "Oh yes, that's great," he called again. Now I spanked him properly and he screamed and moaned with pleasure. This handsome boy was submissive and I took possession of him. I was beside myself and couldn't believe my luck.

A little later I stood in front of him again and said: "And now caress my breasts and suck my mouth on the nipples." Which he immediately did. "Is that a good thing?" He asked. "Yes, you can suck on it a little harder. Lick them with your tongue. "I noticed how hard he tried to follow my instructions. It was magical and he learned quickly. I got more and more excited. Luca was trying so hard to get everything right that his erection had subsided a little. But that didn't bother me at that moment. I lay down with my back on the soft carpet: "Now come and caress my labia. Then put your fingers through the vagina and when you have found the clitoris, rub it. "He also followed this conscientiously. I saw his member slowly rise to full size again and fell into ecstasy. Circled my pelvis and lifted it. Since he noticed how I liked it, he no longer held back and pressed lightly on my clitoris and rubbed it more and more passionately. "Yes, that's a good thing." I breathed excitedly. Now come on, lie on top of me When he was on top of me, we kissed. I took his member in hand and first moved his large glans between my labia. "And now carefully push him in," I said, while I fixed the position of his member at my opening. I felt something enormous spreading deeper and deeper within me. I felt like it filled my entire body. Hold on, my breath caught. He was moaning loudly. When I believed that he was finally completely inside me, I said with a trembling voice: "And now always carefully up and down. I've never had anything like it in me. When he moved into me with it and I felt that he was digging deeper into it, I screamed with lust. Before long it came inside of me. At the same time, his mighty member twitched a few more times. That started a chain reaction in me. The twitching went through my whole body with intense feelings of happiness. Feelings that rose incessantly and finally triggered a dizzying, tremendous orgasm in me. We both trembled and moaned. Again and again, our bodies collided with each other in ecstatic pleasure. After this unearthly orgasmic experience, we were completely exhausted.

Then we looked happily in the eye and lay down next to each other on the carpet, exhausted but satisfied. After a while, I noticed that I was all sweaty. I saw that Luca was also lying next to me, covered in sweat. "Come on, let's take a shower together," I said. We got up and went to the bathroom. Here I insisted on shaving all over his body. When I ran down his back with my slippery hands and finally reached his firm bottom, I slapped my hand on the tight buttocks in high spirits. He groaned and said pleadingly: "Stop it, otherwise I'll be horny again." "How do you know that I wouldn't like that?" I answered him, slapping his butt twice hard. But after that, I stopped being punished and ran my hand forward. His limb was impressive even when it was flaccid. That's why I spent a long time doing the soaping. I ran my hand firmly up and down on him, kneading it, and always guided my other hand evenly between his legs, along with his sack. It quickly started to get harder again. It was a breathtaking spectacle to see how his huge penis kept getting bigger and bigger. Luca was already breathing heavily. That's when I finished my game.

When we got out of the shower and stood naked in the bathroom, he leaned over the sink and stretched his hot ass forward. "Please spank him again," he said. He'd gotten a taste for it again in the shower. Which I wasn't entirely innocent of. I didn't have to be told that twice. I started spanking him with the palm of my hand. He happily wiggled his tight buttocks, which slowly turned red from my blows. "Yes, harder, harder!" He shouted. I noticed his stiff member swaying back and forth with every movement of his pelvis like an upright pendulum. Now I took it firmly between his legs from behind in my hand, bent it down a little, and drove it up and down again. "Oh, that's awesome. Hit me and milk my hard prick violently. "He called again. I had a firm grip on his member. Part of it, that is, because my hand was too small to grasp it in its full size.

I milked him vigorously while spanking his bum at the same time. He gasped with relish. Suddenly it jerked so hard that I could barely hold on to it. Luca shouted: "I'm dying. I'm dying. "His whole body reared up and his semen then shot out of him. It was an overwhelming event. It got wet again between my legs. Seems like it would have happened to me too.

So when he had calmed down, I stood at the sink with my legs apart. "Come now between my thighs and let your tongue play." He sat back on the floor and pressed his face firmly between my spread legs. Then I felt his tongue penetrate deeper and deeper into me and move inside me. That was insane. I screamed too. "Yes, yes, push yourself in even tighter." He held on to my hips so that he could force his face between my legs. And I opened up as much as possible. I couldn't stop and moaned and croaked. Then it came to me. Then Luca got into the highest ecstasy and he got even wilder and didn't want to stop. This action gave me a permanent orgasm. My body twitched incessantly and my legs gave out. Luca caught me and laid me on the sofa in the living room. He sat down next to me and caressed my excited body. These pats and his calming voice with which he spoke brought me to calm again after a while. What happened to me? The boy had opened Pandora's box in me, only that infinite pleasure poured out of it. Although he was submissive, I felt at his mercy. But that didn't worry me. On the contrary, I was happier than ever in my life.

It was early in the evening. I recovered quickly and we decided to stay together tonight. Twice I felt more ecstatic feelings when he was inside me with his mighty member. We tested all possible positions. I also discovered other parts of Luca's body with which I drove him crazy. He always expected precise instructions from me, which he then followed.

During a longer break, I became curious: "You said that you had experiences with boys during your puberty. Tell me which ones they were? "I also had exciting experiences with Susi and was curious to see how boys enjoy each other. Luca replied: "That is not important." "Yes, if I am to continue teaching you, then I have to know everything about your previous experiences." Then he told me: "My father did not hit me often. But if I did it too colorful, then sometimes he would put me over my knee and spank my bum. Until I was 13 years old and got an erection. After that, he left me alone. "He said with a smile. "But I noticed that it excites me. That's why I asked my best friend at the time to spank my butt sometimes. He saw that my member became stiff and he found that exciting. When he later also experienced his first orgasm, he asked me, after he had spanked me properly, to take his member and to give him a jerk in thanks for his blows. I thought that was only fair. Since I was aroused after the punishment, he was amazed to see my stiff large member, how it also twitched with excitement. Over time, he had great admiration playing with it and also bringing me to orgasm. We always did that when he had to spank my bum. Which was often the case at the time. Especially since he later loved to push my member as deep as he could into his mouth. I was 14 years old then and it wasn't as big as it is today. Of course, what he was doing was awesome. He got crazy about it and couldn't get enough of it to suckle. I think the constant erections that he caused in me over and over again during these two years led to the fact that my penis became so big because of the constant pumping. At this age, it is still in the growth phase. It was probably good training for this huge increase in size. Over time, to the delight of my friend, I developed a great deal of stamina. But then his mother caught us when he was sucking my penis again full of enthusiasm, and he was no longer allowed to be with me. We were both sad about it, but he was too afraid of his parents. So we didn't meet again. However, these bans didn't do him much good, because today he hangs out with an older man all the time and I think they play completely different games with each other. When I met him again a few months ago, he raved about my large member and asked whether it had grown any further. I could confirm that to him. He then asked me if I could meet his friend sometime.

"We will certainly have a lot of fun there. He has a super hot ass that he always wants to have stuffed. "He said. But I didn't know the man. So I turned down this offer. Since then I haven't had a new boyfriend or girlfriend. Castle Luca the story. I was happy about his honesty and therefore told him about Susi and me. Luca found that very interesting and was by no means against it. We became a couple and understood each other, sexually and humanly, as well as two people can understand each other.

He was only submissive during sex. The friendship between Susi and me remained unbroken. With her, I enjoyed the tenderness that only women can give one another. Luca knew about it and since Susi was also curious about his powerful member, which I had enthusiastically told her about and wanted to experience his submissive lust for himself, the three of us had our fun now and then. When Luca had watched Susi and I enjoy being together a few times, he too wanted to try it out with a boy again. With his appearance and figure, it was certainly not difficult for him to find a suitable partner. And lo and behold, a short time later he arrived with Erik, the crush of all girls and Susi's previous date. At first, Susi was appalled by it. But when she had spoken to Erik and he confessed to her: "You know, back then in the cinema I saw the boys next to us stroking each other's ever-growing bumps between their legs and at that moment I felt so much wish I were one of the two. I was so shocked about that and wanted to prove to myself that I am not like that. That's why I pushed you so hard afterward. I'm sorry, Susi. "Then she realized that he had only played the daredevil back then to suppress his natural desires. She could understand him and over time they became very human. Often the four of us were now playing our love games. Erik loved to spank Luca's bottom properly and then penetrate him. But over time I got the taste for taking in the large member of him. When Luca carefully pushed his powerful device into him, he moaned and whimpered continuously with lust. It drives him crazy as much as it does me, I thought.

It was great to see two such pretty boys enjoying each other with relish. And they also enjoyed watching the love game between Susi and me. Thank goodness Luca was very potent, so I didn't miss out either. Erik and Susi also became a couple. So the four of us had a happy time together and enjoyed it to the full.

***

Drawing folder "Der Liebesreigen"
-Miniature excerpt 3-

4. Best friends

"And now, ladies and gentlemen, watch out!" The math teacher gave us another example from probability theory on the blackboard. At every opportunity, he tried to show us that it could predict future events. Nobody understood this gibberish anyway, but it was his favorite subject and we let it go. Besides, I didn't get the point. Why should I calculate the events in advance? Where would the tension be if I knew what was going to happen in advance? When I looked around, I saw that everyone was busy with something else and not listening, which was of no further interest to Mr. Müller, our math teacher. Suddenly I felt Peer's warm hand on my thighs again, gently sliding higher and higher. Peer and I were best friends.

He had only come to our class a year ago and we hit it off right away. He was a handsome and very friendly boy and had many admirers from my classmates. However, he was a bit shy, at least towards the girls. Some boys also sought closer contact with him. He was often asked whether he wanted to come with us for a swim or into town. He always turned to me and asked me: "Do we want to go with you?" If I didn't feel like it, he canceled. Sometimes I had the feeling that he was happy about it and liked to be alone with me. That flattered me. We sat together in the middle row on the last bench. In that row, she was behind everyone else. So we always had a complete overview of the classroom. That had another advantage for us.

Nobody could see what we were doing under the bench. Now we were in the 10th grade. Peer often strokes my thighs during class, like at this moment.

I had only experienced this once before, when I was in eighth grade, with an older boy who attended my school but was two years older. We met by chance at the lake and were there alone. He caressed my stiff member as I lay there. I couldn't move. I had my first ejaculation a few weeks earlier in my sleep. Now it was getting stuff all the time, like at that moment when I was lying at the lake. The boy saw that too and sat down next to me. It was completely new to me and I was horny as soon as he touched me and then quickly squirted off. He arranged to meet me again. I only knew him by sight before. I soon realized that he was only interested in me and himself. I liked that, but he wasn't interested in me. We always met secretly. And nobody at school should notice that we know each other.

It made me uncomfortable. Therefore, after a while, I refused his constant requests to meet him at the lake. Finally, he gave up on pushing me further.

It was different with Peer. We were friends. After a while, Peer slowly ran his hand upwards until it reached my crotch. He wanted to see if I had an erection yet. Of course, I did. When he got to the top and gently caressed my large bump, I had to suppress an audible moan. Today I was wearing baggy trousers and my member was gradually able to make room in them. So it was soon there in its full size. That made my boyfriend not let go of him anymore. Excited, my hard stick reared up all the time now. Since he kept going up and down on him with his hand, it became too much for me, because I was afraid of getting a damp, visible stain in my pants. That would have been embarrassing. Although Peer had excited me a lot and I was about to surrender to my fate, I pulled myself together at the last minute, took his hand, and pushed it away. But since he noticed how sharp I had become, he didn't want to stop. To distract him I now quickly ran my hand along his thigh, all the way to the top, and scared at the already considerably large bump in his pants. I kept my hand away from him. He also got an erection and had a large member. It started twitching and jumping as I gently stroked it through his pants. Peer's face always had a magical aura when he got horny. It was always an exciting experience for me and for him too. He let go of me and surrendered to his fate. Although he no longer had his hand in my crotch, I was already so excited that my penis continued to twitch when I felt him move more and more vigorously. I didn't want to stop then either. But since I had to fear that he would cum soon, I stopped doing it. But Peer whispered: "Go on." "But when you come, your pants will get wet," I answered. "That won't happen," he said. Since I liked to see him so excited, I put my hand back on his member and stroked it evenly up and down. I looked into his face and saw him roll his eyes. His member reared up and I suddenly felt a tremendous twitch. He sat very stiffly and gritted his teeth. It came to him. I was on the verge of it too, but I managed to hold it back just barely. Suddenly it was over and he looked at me with shining eyes. "That was insane," he said. "You have to experience that too. It's your turn in the next hour. "Then he told me: „I put a condom on my penis beforehand. So that the pants don't get wet. "

In the next break, I ran to the toilet and also put on a condom that he had given me. Right after class started, I felt his hand gently slide up and down between my legs. The action in the last hour with him had already aroused me and I got an erection immediately. Now Peer wouldn't let go of him. He kept running his fingers along my penis. I got horny and had to pull myself together so that nobody would notice. Over time, this excitement became almost unbearable. "Take the whole hand and drive along with it faster," I whispered to him. He enjoyed my horniness, just as I enjoyed his, and wanted to keep it as long as possible.

So he asked: "Why, don't you like it that much?" "Of course I like it, but I can't take it anymore without making a sound. Please do it faster. I finally want to cum." Peer answered my plea and now ran his hand incessantly along with my already violently twitching member. My whole body started shaking from within. Because I had to suppress the steadily increasing excitement, I believed that I would soon lose consciousness. I saw all of them blurred and my head was spinning. It finally came out of me tremendously. Clenching my teeth didn't help. I groaned loudly. However, I was able to turn it into a loud sneeze. "Sorry," I said to the teacher who looked at me. During the break, I threw away the condom. I didn't have a stain.

Peer loved it, and I loved it too. Still, I asked him not to do that in class anymore. I was afraid that the others in our class might notice it over time. Worse still the teachers would surely tell the parents. Peer saw that. So it stayed with the constant petting under the bench, without it coming to us and that was also very exciting.

A short time later he asked me: "My parents are going to see my aunt for two days. Wouldn't it be great if you stayed with me during this time? "At first I was surprised because we haven't been to each other's apartment very often. At most briefly, when one of us picked the other up from home. But when I looked into his shining eyes, I knew what he was getting at.

My stomach started tingling at this thought. "I'll talk to my parents. But I don't think they mind. "I answered.

Peer beamed at me. "That will be awesome. Imagine the two of us all alone for two days. "Again I had a feeling of construction and was looking forward to it as well. Then on Friday after school, we ran to Peer together. His parents hadn't left yet but wanted to leave straight away. His mother quickly showed us where the food she had prepared for us was. "You have to eat like this. So have a nice weekend. And no girls overnight, please. "She said and laughed.

When they were gone, Peer first took out the beer he had hidden. We lounged on the sofa and drank our beer like the grown-ups.

Neither of us had kissed a girl before. We didn't know how to kiss properly. When we talked about it, Peer said, "Let's try it. Maybe we'll find out on our own. "The kissing thing was also important to me. I've had the opportunity to visit a girl a couple of times. But I kept backing down because I didn't want to admit that I hadn't had any experience with it. "Yes, we will manage that," I answer. And so we pressed our lips together and pushed our tongue forward. After the first unsuccessful attempt, we did better the second time. After that, we continued to practice and over time we liked it extraordinarily well. Peer put his hand between my legs and I followed suit. We quickly got horny with it. "We're all alone here. Here bothers and nobody. We should take off our clothes, otherwise, we will get stains on our pants. "Said, Peer. That made sense, so I agreed.

We took off our things and faced each other naked. We both had an erection. Peer's penis was bigger than mine. I took it in my hand full of admiration: "It's powerful. I want one too. "

And he replied: "You will surely get that. I heard it can grow up to your 25th year. So you still have nine years for it. "Since I continued to hold its stiff member in my hand while we were talking, it began to move again. So I ran my hand along with it. "Wait," Peer called. "Let's orgasm together while we kiss. That's nicer. "He came over to me and pressed his body against mine. Then we kissed. I felt the big limb of him on my stomach. As if by ourselves we began to rub our bodies and especially the aroused limbs together. We got harder and faster. We kissed. Peer began to shiver and shouted: "I'll be right there." To feel his body tightly embraced by mine, in this trembling excitement, also led me to a climax and the semen came out at the same time, with loud moans of lust shot us out. We were overwhelmed by these feelings. When we parted our bodies, both bellies were wet from the heavy ejaculation that had seized us. So I ran into the bathroom under the shower and lathered each other off. We were both very active on the soccer team and had a sporty figure. When I got to his tight little bottom, he said: "Yes, I like that. Go through my furrow. "

I gladly followed this invitation, because I felt how it aroused him. That's why I stayed there for a while and always run my hand through his buttocks. Peer bent down so I could go deeper. When I ran my fingers over his hole, he whispered, "Oh that's awesome." That piqued my curiosity. "Come on, now it's my turn," I said to him and he did not take long to ask. Immediately he ran his hand through my column as well. "Bend over." He asked me. I immediately followed this request. So, with the soap in his hand, he always slid along inside her. It excites me and I bent lower so that Peer could get to my hole even better. With his index finger, he tickled it now and I whimpered with pleasure. "Oh, that way you can spoil me for hours." I cried. But he soon stopped and said, "Come on let's go into the room. We oil each other there and explore all parts of our bodies. That sounded promising and I ran into the other room with him.

He took a large bottle of the body oil from the closet. I suspected that he had prepared everything beforehand and I was happy about it. He took the oil and we rubbed each other. First, he started doing it with me. "You have beautiful, soft skin," he said while sliding his oily hand carefully over her.

As was to be expected, he took a long time to oil my member, so that it became stiff again. But this time it suddenly stopped, which surprised me. "Why are you stopping?" I asked him. "We have time and can try out whatever else we like." "Okay," I answered him, but again had the feeling that he was pursuing a certain goal. When he was finished on my front side and the abundantly applied oil was shiny on the skin, he asked me: "First of all, oil my back and buttocks." He immediately bent down and spread his legs so that the buttocks opened wide. I saw its glowing pink bud. That excited me and I accepted this invitation. Ran his hand through his furrow and tickled his hole just like he'd done me before. He moaned and protested again and again how cool it was. "Carefully stick a finger in me." He asked. I also liked to follow that, because when I rubbed his hole hard, the idea was already floating through my head. So I carefully stuck my index finger in it and wiggled it when I was inside. He whimpered and groaned. "Yes, go out a little and then back in." As I did that, I noticed how it was gradually getting warmer inside him. "Take two fingers." He asked me a short time later. Now I took my index and middle finger and he groaned louder as I slowly drove it into him. That means, always a little bit out and in again with both fingers. Peer fell into ecstasy. He moved his hot little bum back and forth and shouted: "Yes, yes, go on." His hole became warm and moist. "Lower now," he called. "My fingers are already all the way in. I don't get any deeper with it. "I said to him. "Then take your member and stick it in." He urged me excitedly. I've had a boner the whole time. So I gently pushed him into his hole. The loud whimpers and moans from him told me that he liked it very much. I felt my member slowly slide into it and it didn't want to end until it was completely inside. It was pleasantly warm and soft there. "Now move. Ride me with your hard member. "I watched how he always moved his hot ass back and forth and moaned loudly with excitement. He was beside himself and moving it faster and faster. I had never seen him so hot. I would have loved to stay in there forever, but soon an orgasm pushed itself up in me and I rode him now in wild desperation to finally find redemption. It came to me and when Peer felt my semen splash into him he also got louder and more aroused.

After that my member fell asleep again, I would have liked to continue to do it with him. "Oh, that was so cool. We have to repeat that as often as possible. "He exclaimed enthusiastically." But now you too should feel this indescribable feeling, come bend down." I leaned forward and held on to the table.

He rubbed my butt and my hole with plenty of oil for a long time. As he massaged me harder and harder, I was horny too and I opened my buttocks as far as I could. Then he came with his member to introduce it to me. But it was so big that I tensed up and it hurt. He pulled it out of me again. "Please relax, you will see, it works and then it is indescribably beautiful. Believe me. "I was more relaxed on the second try.

Probably also because he kept whispering to me: "Stay relaxed. It's so wonderful how you open up. Oh my god, your bum is so hot. Yes, push my member into you. "And before I knew it, it was inside me. At first, it was strange for me to have something strange in there. But when he slowly slipped in and out of me, it aroused me more and more. In the end, I got beside myself and moved my bottom rhythmically. Lower, lower than I called. Until he was completely within me with his large member. Then he rode me hard and I roared with pleasure. Oh, how beautiful love can be, I thought. I couldn't quite believe it yet. I had never even dreamed of something so exciting. But I felt it and I was bursting with happiness. Yes, there was something great and I experienced it at that moment. But soon he came to him and I felt how his member reared itself violently in me several times. After that, it quickly went limp and slipped out of me. I was a little disappointed with that. But then I thought, we'll be together for two more days, so we'll have the opportunity to repeat that.

Now we ran into the kitchen because we were hungry. His mother bought pizza for us. We put them on the stove and baked them. While we were waiting, we drank the second beer and kissed now and then. Then the pizza was ready and we pounced on it hungrily. Thank God it was an XXL format and we were both fed up. After we had satiated ourselves and sat together, we ran into the shower again, because we were still sweaty from the ecstatic associations that were behind us. When we had cleaned ourselves up properly, Peer said full of energy: "And now we're starting the next round." "I don't know if he's going to stiffen up again. Maybe we should take a longer break. "I said, a little uncertain. But he replied: "Wait a minute, I have an idea." He crouched down in front of me and I noticed how he took my member in his mouth. Then he tickled the glans more and more with his tongue. I got excited again and got an erection again. What he was doing to me was so wonderful. I would have liked to have wanted him to continue until it squirts out ... But Peer wanted to get his money's worth too. And well, in his hole was at least as beautiful as his mouth, I thought. He had already opened wide and held out his willing buttocks to me. So I pushed my hard member into him full of joy. This time I had more stamina. After all, it was the third time within two hours. Peer was delighted with this long ride. He also learned quickly and the movements with his backside became more and more provocative. Finally, it came to me. I had never experienced three highlights in one day, let alone within two hours. But that wasn't supposed to happen for the last time that day either, which I didn't know yet.

I felt amazing. Immediately Peer said: "Come on, you put my member in your mouth." I was still asleep and I was able to take it into my mouth. It quickly got bigger inside, so that I had to take it in my hand and could only push it halfway in. I also licked his glans with my tongue. And since he kept shouting how wonderful it is, I moved her faster and harder on her. How exciting it was to hear him moan loudly with lust.

Since his member was bigger than mine and I noticed with regret that my hole hurt a bit from the last time, I didn't necessarily want to feel it inside me again. So I just kept licking so that he could no longer have a clear thought, but just moaned loudly. He was delivered to me and let everything go through willingly until another orgasm seized him. After he had calmed down, he exclaimed enthusiastically, "What was that! You have to do that more often. "I smiled." What is that?" I asked jokingly.

Peer was overwhelmed with excitement. We continued to play these and similar games over the next two days and nights with a lot of joy and imagination. After that, we were completely exhausted. It was good that his parents came back after two days because I didn't think we could have stopped doing this on our own any longer. After this weekend we use every opportunity to have fun together. We founded a learning community for two as an alibi. So our parents thought nothing of it when they often found us in the room after school.

A few months later I met Anna and discovered how exciting it can be with a girl. She ran into me during the school sports festival. Peer was sick, so he wasn't there. So sometimes I stood alone on the pitch.

She took this opportunity and spoke to me. She asked me: "Would you like to have an ice cream with me and the others afterward?" Anna was very pretty and I had noticed that she often adored Peer. Surely she wants to get up to me to ask about him, I thought. But since I had nothing better to do at the moment, I said yes.

When we were sitting together in the ice cream parlor, she asked me if I would like to go to the cinema with her tomorrow. I looked at her in disbelief. "You keep adoring Peer, why do you want to go to the cinema with me?" I asked. "I don't adore Peer. I look to you all the time. But you're always together, so I inevitably see him. "She answered me. "Then I got it wrong. If I had noticed beforehand that you meant me, then I would have spoken to you a long time ago. "Anna beamed at me and said: "Well, now it's cleared up. „ And kissed me on the mouth. "I like that," I whispered and she came to me with her pretty face and we kissed properly. It was a good thing I'd practiced it enough with Peer, I thought. Now I could show it off. When her friends saw that we were kissing, they shouted: "Finally!" Anna had already told them about her interest in me.

Soon afterward we said goodbye to her friends, because we wanted to be a little alone, and ran to the nearby park.

There we found a sheltered place, hugged each other, and kissed each other tightly. This excited me and my member became stiff. Eva saw it and said, "It seems pretty big." I was just able to hold back because it was on the tip of my tongue to say that Peer's is much bigger. I kept kissing her, caressing her breasts.

She unbuttoned her blouse a bit, showing me that I can go in. She didn't have a bra on and so I felt the bare skin and her nipples, which were already stiff. Since I noticed how aroused her when I ran my hand over her nipples, I rubbed them gently. She groaned and reached with her hand through my pants to my member. The harder I rubbed her nipples, the harder she ran her hand along the penis. We kissed and moaned softly so that no one could hear us. An orgasm slowly began to develop in me, which I felt in my constantly increasing excitement, while Anna incessantly moved her hand up and down my penis. I had to fear that I would soon get damp. That's why I got him out. At first, she was a little frightened, but I said: "Come on, carry on." While I rubbed her nipples vigorously, she caressed my member. Go downstairs too, she whispered excitedly. I wasn't told twice. I ran my hand under her skirt and into her panties. Her labia were wonderfully soft and when I slipped my fingers between them, it was warm and moist.

She moaned a little louder and I was afraid that we would be discovered. But then she took my member tightly in her hand and continued, getting more and more violent. An irrepressible lust rose in me. I stuck a finger in her hole in excitement. Always in and out, in the same rhythm as she drove up and down my member. It wasn't long before I felt a tremendous orgasm rob my senses. I came and shouted. That could not be avoided. I quickly took my finger out of her again and put the still hard member in my pants. I was afraid that passers-by would come to see what happened. Eva lay on the grass with wet eyes and I leaned over her. We kissed again. "That was so nice," I said to her. "Yes, for me too." She answered and continued: "Next time we will meet in a place where nobody will bother us." I was happy that she was thinking about the next time and said quickly. "We can meet at my place. My parents don't come home until five o'clock. "I often met Peer at my home after school. "Then we'll go to you tomorrow. You got me excited I'm looking forward to it. "She said.

The next day, Peer was still ill, I ran to see Anna with Anna straight away after school. As soon as we were in my room, we kissed hard and then undressed each other. My love arrow was already standing in front of her in all its glory and Anna marveled at it. When she reached for it with my hand, I fought it off and kissed it. I wanted to avoid having to cum so quickly again. At first, I planned to research it extensively. "Come on, lie down," I said and she lay on her back. Now I kissed her and laid my body on top of her. Then I slid down until I got to her breasts. Her nipples were hard again. I sucked on it with my lips and Anna was moaning loudly. A short time later I pushed my body further down and kissed her on her book. Then slid even lower until my head was between her legs. I marveled at her labia, which had already opened a bit, full of curiosity. I ran my finger up and down between them. Then I saw how her clit came out and got bigger and bigger. I then rubbed it. Anna groaned and lifted her pelvis a little. That was exciting. I rubbed it faster and faster, which caused her to moan incessantly. "You can stick it in if you want. I crawled up to her again with my body and stuck my member inside her. Immediately she raised her pelvis, moving. I tried to follow her. These were movements that I knew well from Peer. Just from the other side. Suddenly she was trembling all over and I soon reached my climax too. We both moaned together so loudly as if one wanted to drown out the other. When it came to me, I was moving like crazy inside her, trying to prolong my orgasm. She had her hips swung as high as she could. But finally, she collapsed and lay exhausted under me. She opened her eyes: "I've never seen anything like it. I love you. "She said, caressing me tenderly. I was also bewitched: "I love you too." I answered. After we had settled down a bit, we took a shower and soap off each other. We were able to explore our bodies further. When it reached my bottom and ran through the furrow over my hole, I opened it and moaned softly, as I was used to with my boyfriend. "Does a boy like it when you stroke his hole?" She asked. "Why not?" I answered. "Well, I'll be happy to do that next time, because I've always loved your butt. I would definitely like that. " Me too, „I said happily. The next day at school, she must have told her friends about our date. At first, I didn't like that she had to tell it all over the place, but suddenly most of them looked at me in admiration. I was the star of the class that day. Some boys then tried to talk to me and wanted to know how it was and what I had done. But that wasn't my way of talking about it. Anna and I were officially a couple. We ran to my house every day after school and let our imaginations run wild. Tried every position we knew about and then managed to climax mostly twice in the afternoon by the time my parents came home.

She noticed something, but didn't question me. I only noticed that my father was quite proud of me because I had such a beautiful girlfriend. Would he have been proud if he had known what I was doing with Peer in my room for a long time, I thought and had to smile. Once Anna brought a dildo. She showed it to me and said: "I still have it from before we were together. But even then I had always thought of you when I used it. "I became curious." Show me how you can satisfy yourself with it." I asked her. She slowly guided him into her hole as he vibrated. Always a bit out and then in again. I saw on her face that it aroused her. "Go ahead," I said, starting to rub her nipples. She got faster with her dildo. It had several levels of vibration because I heard it getting louder and louder. I took her breasts and put my member between them. Then I squeezed her together, continuing to play with her nipples while moving my penis in the crevice that had formed. During this time she pushed her dildo further in and out. She tipped her head back and moaned loudly. Sometimes I would turn my head back to see how she used the vibrating part inside of her. These exciting observations distracted me from my own rising horniness. Then it came back to her and she got completely wet in the crotch. I stopped sliding my member between her breasts. She pushed the dildo out of herself and handed it to me. "Do you want to try it too? She asked. I stood and bent down. Then I carefully pushed it inside me. I didn't find that particularly nice. When Anna noticed this in the expression on my face, she said, "You have to turn on the vibration." Which I then did. But such a strange device in me was not my cup of tea. Peer's beating was different, because there was a whole guy on it, whose excitement I felt and that excited me completely. So I pushed the dildo out of me and gave it back to her. "No, that doesn't turn me on. But if you do it with yourself, then I'll get wild watching too. "I said. After an hour she was ready to show me again. Now I was watching her more closely. I stood with my back across her legs apart and ran my hand along my penis as I watched her rise in excitement. I already knew this position from my friend Peer. Who asked me every now and then that I jerk off while he was standing over me with his legs apart and was doing a lot of work on his member himself. We watched each other. I looked from below at his firm bottom and at the testicles, how they rocked back and forth. He watched my member, how it twitched and in the end the semen shot out of it. That was always exciting and exciting for us. But often I couldn't take it to the end. His hot ass drove me so crazy that I got up in the middle and took him from behind to come to a happy ending. Which Peer happily endured with grunts and moans every time. Anna had already set the dildo to full vibration level and led it violently in and out as far as it would go. She moaned loudly. That excited me too and I drove harder and faster along my pleasure injection. Then I came and injected the love juice on her body below, trembling with ecstasy. I kept swinging my member back and forth so that she could feel my semen all over the place. She called: "Yes, yes. That's wonderful.

"And then it came to her too. When we said goodbye that day, Anna left her dildo with me so she could continue to use it for my pleasure every now and then. In the evening in bed I tried again on myself. This time I imagined Peer penetrating me with lust and moaning. As I saw the images in my imagination, I pushed the dildo in and out of me. I liked it better then. After two weeks, Peer came back to school. He had been sick longer than expected. So I was all the more happy to finally see him again. I greeted him with bright eyes, but he stayed cool. At first I thought who knows what he's got. He'll catch himself again. But when he was still dismissive after a while, I asked him during the break: "What's the matter with you? You're so weird.,, I thought you'd come and see me when I'm sick for so long," he said. He was right and I felt guilty. "Sorry, but I've been so busy ..." "I know." He cut me off. "You're with Anna now, so of course you didn't have time for your best friend." I'm so sorry. Are you okay again? "You can see that," he replied briefly. We sat side by side in class all day long. It was almost unbearable because I was really looking forward to seeing him again. But I understood him too. The next day I asked him if he would like to do something with me on Saturday. "Not until Saturday?" He replied. "Yes, Eva doesn't have time. We could be together all day. " Even so, Eva doesn't have time. But I also don't know if I have time. I wanted to go swimming with a few friends. "In fact, he went to the lake with some schoolmates on Saturday. He didn't ask me if I want to come with him. Only the others did that, because they knew we were friends. But that wasn't enough for me. So I stayed home alone. Of course, the activities under the school desk were also canceled. He didn't touch me anymore. Still, I sometimes got horny when I saw him sitting next to me with his legs apart and looking at the bulge in his pants. Even when he was running in front of me, I sometimes imagined how I stroked his hot little bottom and he got wild again. When I tried it with him under the bench and put my hand carefully on his thigh, he said: "Come on, don't do that. It's no use. " What do you mean? What purpose? "I asked, puzzled. But he didn't answer and just shook his head. He soon had a new boyfriend who was two grades above us in school. It was the same one who first brought me to orgasm. In other words, it wasn't a real friend for Peer either. I saw that they weren't standing together in school. He probably had the same meetings with him that he wanted to have with me back then. Whenever he told Peer that he wanted to meet him, he was happy about it and ran to him, even if he had planned something else beforehand. This boy stayed in town after graduating from school and they continued to meet. After two years, our school days were also coming to an end. We had all passed our final exams and I had applied to study veterinary medicine at agricultural school. Anna studied at the UNI in Leipzig. So it would mean saying goodbye for us. We wanted to stay together and have a long-distance relationship, but actually neither of us really believed that it would work. I didn't know what Peer was up to. He didn't talk to anyone about it. One day he suddenly stood next to me in the school yard and spoke to me. "I would like to invite you to my place on the weekend. My parents are not there and we could speak properly again before we lose sight of each other completely. After all, we were friends once. "I hadn't expected it anymore, but I was very happy about it. Although I had an appointment with Anna, I said yes and she said no. This time I didn't want to screw it up again. The next day I stood in front of his apartment door. My heart pounded with excitement. I bravely rang the bell and Peer opened the door for me. His parents were already gone. "Come sit down. Do you want a beer? " "Yes, I would. „I said. He got two bottles of beer out of the fridge and we toasted glasses. "To our future." I toasted him and saw how Peer didn't move a mine. Then he looked at me with his faithful dog eyes, which I knew well and had missed so much. "Oh Peer." I said and we kissed. "You are my best friend and it will always be like that," Peer said excitedly. And the tears ran down his pretty face. I kissed her away and replied, "I'm so sorry I was such an idiot at the time. I didn't understand that I hurt you so much with my behavior. Please excuse me. "And then tears came to me too. We hugged and kissed and couldn't part anymore. We quickly undressed and rubbed our naked, excited bodies hard and wild against each other. "I missed you so much," he said. "I've had an insane yearning for you so often." I replied back. And that made us even more ecstatic. I quickly turned and bent down. Come on, I want to feel you inside of me again. And he drove into me. It came to him soon after. "Please don't stop," I begged him and he just kept going. I supported him with all my might, moving my butt back and forth as fast as I could. Slowly I felt how his member in me became hard again and Peer groaned: "I love you so much. I've loved you all along. "He exclaimed. He then rode me for at least half an hour. When he was done, I said "And now it's my turn" He beamed at me and crouched down. He lifted his tight bum and I was completely crazy to finally take possession of him again. I quickly drove into him and he called: "Oh, that's nice. You're back. "With his ride inside me he had overwhelmed me so much that, to his delight, it took a long time until an orgasm overwhelmed me. Exhausted, we fell to the side and we looked happily into each other's eyes. "Peer, I really want to continue, but I need a break." He looked at me lovingly: "Don't worry. We do everything you want today and as often as you want. "Then we ate and drank something. Strengthened, we made passionate love again a short time later and gradually took up all the positions that we had tried earlier. But at some point even the best will no longer helps, and neither does the greatest desire. We needed a longer break. We made spaghetti with tomato sauce in the kitchen. Our heads slowly became clearer again. Peer was the best person to talk about uncomfortable things when he was busy doing other things. I used this quality even then when he was hiding something from me or when he couldn't really get out of the language. I then looked for something to do for us and he became talkative and told me what

I wanted to know. I was already amused at the time how easy it was to get everything out of him if you know how. But that's why I loved him too. I wanted to use today's cooking together in the kitchen to find out more about his plans. I asked him if he was still seeing this boy he'd been with for the past two years. "Yes." He said. "But he'll only call me if he'd like to fuck me anyway." I was startled. "But Peer, that's bullshit. Why do you put up with that? " Well, it's just great when we're together, and I don't know anyone else either. " And what are you going to do after school? "I asked. "It used to be my goal to study, but then I would no longer be here and I would also lose my last friend. That's why I'm thinking of starting an apprenticeship as a machine fitter in town. " You really plan to stay here because of these boys and ruin your whole future? „I asked him. "I know that's not optimal and my parents are mad at me because of that." He replied. "Do you love him then?" I asked further. "I don't know," he said thoughtfully. "Actually, he always only wants one thing and otherwise has no time for me. Love? I don't think I love him and he doesn't love me either. Although he always says it, but only during sex and it's very good, but after that I'm written off for him for the time being. Until he gets horny again and agrees to meet me again. " Then stick to your goal of studying. You are such a great young man, you will definitely find a better friend or friends there. "Then something occurred to me: "Do you remember how we always dreamed of a farm back then? "Yes, a farm, that is still my greatest wish." He confirmed. "Then study with me at the agricultural school. There are still places available. "I said to him „Studying with you would be great," he replied. "And I would be happy too. Imagine the two of us together in a student dorm. "I said. He beamed at me. Suddenly he looked sad again. "But when you have a new girlfriend, you leave me alone again." "Peer, I promise you that I will never let you down like I did then. We'll always be best friends, but don't worry if I have a new girlfriend. Maybe you will find a friend there who is also not interested in girls and just wants to be with you. It can happen that you don't have that much time for me anymore. But maybe you are interested in a girl after all. I love you too and can still be happy with a girl too. But no matter which way we go, we always remain friends. "Peer's face brightened up and he said, "You are right, we are studying together at the agricultural school. „Then we hugged and kissed. And had all night to reseal our friendship. It was not a wild night, but a tender and sensual one. We talked in between and forged many plans together until morning came.

5. Book Recommendation

Noh Fakier- www.noahfakier.eu –
Drawing folder "Der Liebesreigen" for the book
Driven by the deep need

With 18 drawings

Erotic drawings about the wonderful diversity of love. The first drawing portfolio by Noah Fakier-Männer I has already attracted international attention and has become a bestseller at BoD Verlag. It can be assumed that Der Liebesreigen, with its expressive drawings, builds on this. The  representation of physical love is not shown here in pornography but in all its exciting and natural beauty. The drawings are offered in high quality on 200g paper in brilliant print and a ring binder for German collectors. A quality that pays off. Each drawing can also be separated individually. For organizational reasons, there is also a second variant, mainly for the foreign market, on 90g paper in brilliant print in bound

form. Which is of course also available in Germany. You can get there by clicking on Noah Fakier you can find the best presentation on:
ISBN: 9783749498475

Noah Fakier- www.noahfakier.eu -
The secret stories from 1001 nights

I dedicate this book to the victims who are still threatened with the death penalty for their love. The stories in this book are for all people who are free from prejudice and want to learn more about love and lust among men. There are many poems from the ancient Orient that tell about it. That was a tradition for over a thousand years. And everyone was pleased. Today all kinds of love are recognized in many countries. Only the Orient plays an inglorious role in this. In doing so, he questions his rich human history. This book ties in with the ancient traditions of the Orient. Life intolerance was a strength of the empire at that time. The true size of a country is shown in the freedom and happiness of its people who live in it. There is no substitute for money or wealth. It was like that in earlier times and it always will be. One can only hope that humanity will win again in the Orient. It's not just about abolishing the

death penalty for men who love each other. It is about the freedom of all people to be able to live in love and be happy. This is a fundamental law of humanity that goes far beyond all religions in the world.
ISDN: 9783753462233

Drawings from:
The secret stories from 1001 nights

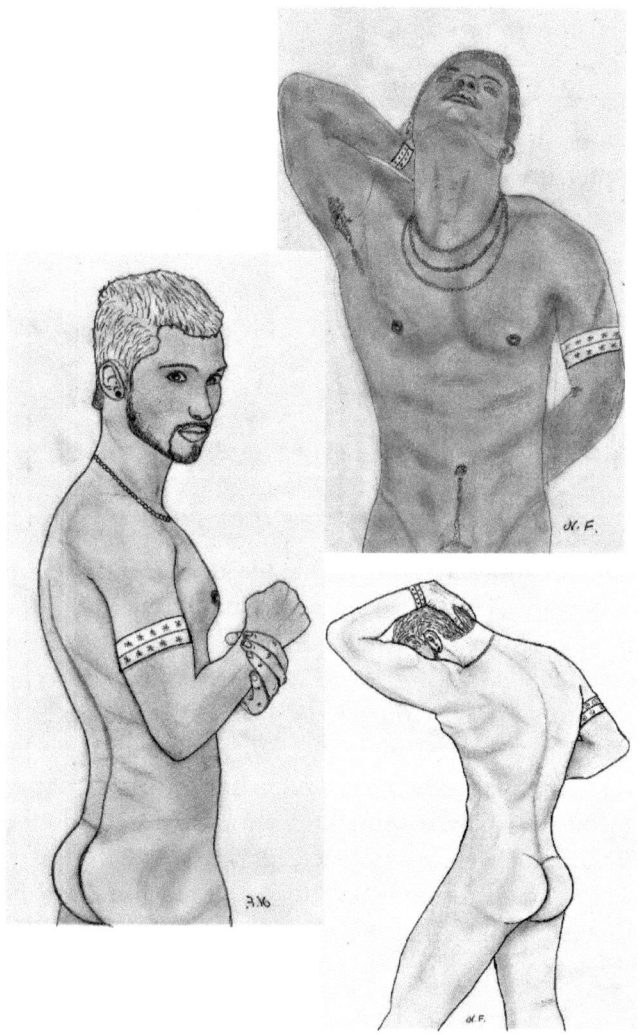

Dr. Lutz Knoche – www.lutzknoche.com -
Book Description Traumata Part I

If you write about
sex openly or speak
publicly, most
people feel bad
about it. What is
going on? Why are
the strongest and
most beautiful
feelings so
embarrassing for
most of the
world? You can give
us a lot of joy and
vitality. You don't
talk about it because
of morality? What

kind of morality and who made it? Do we have to
follow this, even if we feel and think differently? What
if our dreams and fantasies look completely
different? How honest do we deal with it? Or to put
it another way, why are we lying to ourselves? To
adapt to so-called morality? Why has man been put
into a sexual straitjacket and ashamed of his natural
feelings? There is something wrong. More and more
divorces, marriage violence, dramatic events due to
jealousy and relationship stress, and much more show
that something has to change fundamentally. The
book answered these questions and made readers

think. It can be the first step towards a new, happy future.

The book, Traumata of Mankind Part I Trauma Sex ", is even for Dr. Lutz Knoche a very special book. He has been dealing with this topic for years, which he also encountered more and more frequently in his practical work. He carried out a lot of spectacular research and targeted interviews and group discussions, which have found their way into this book.

ISBN 9783753442785

Dr. Lutz Knoche- www.lutzknoche.com -
Luck is not a coincidence- Positive thinking is not
enough

Man strives for a
happy and fulfilling
life. They are trying,
and some are
working very hard
on it. But you don't
seem to be quite
succeeding. I got to
know a lot of people.
Very few were
satisfied and happy,
despite many
positive thoughts
and wishes. Why is
that? In this book,
you will find out

which thoughts, feelings, and actions, which have so
far mostly remained undetected, keep you from
fulfilling your wishes. You will learn how you can
change these thoughts and feelings and thus set the
course for wish fulfillment. Read how to correctly
formulate your wishes so that they can be heard. Walk
the path to a new level of consciousness under
guidance. Read which simple method helps you to
achieve your goals. You will learn step by step what
you have to do to make your wishes like love,
happiness, health, and success come true. Enter the
existential world of yourself, where body, thinking,

feelings, consciousness, and universal consciousness form a unity. For the first time, an extremely effective prayer is presented in this book, with which you can achieve success even faster.
ISBN: 9783753442594

Dr. Lutz Knoche- www.lutzknoche.com - Video Bioenergetics massage

Stress and traumatic experiences also manifest themselves physically. Energy blockages arise.
Blockages that can weaken our body considerably.

The video shows you how you can remedy these disorders or significantly increase your general well-being. Suitable for private use or as a professional massage training.

It will be available on CD from July 2021. Duration approx. 90 minutes,

Price: € 29.95

Order and payment via PayPal